PHOTO BY JEROME ANDERSON

Carl L. Biemiller has long been a familiar name to magazine readers, and to a continually growing audience of juvenile fiction fans. He has been a journalist most of his life, a former assistant publisher of the Camden *Courier-Post* and the Philadelphia *Daily News,* a long time executive editor of Holiday Magazine. He lives on the New Jersey coast within the sound of the surf, and his interest in oceanography is always at high tide. He works today in the public relations business between books. When this one was written he was serving as public relations director for the City of Atlantic City, and planning another volume for his *Hydronaut* series.

Follow
the
Whales

Books by Carl L. Biemiller

The Albino Blue
The Hydronauts
Follow the Whales

CARL L. BIEMILLER

Follow the Whales
The HYDRONAUTS Meet the Otter-People

DOUBLEDAY & COMPANY, INC., GARDEN CITY, NEW YORK

ISBN: 0-385-01660-3 Trade
 0-385-02387-1 Prebound
Library of Congress Catalog Card Number 72-92190
Copyright © 1973 by Carl L. Biemiller
All Rights Reserved
Printed in the United States of America
First Edition

Acknowledgments: This is a work of science fiction, and fiction only. Nevertheless the author is grateful for the use of such works as *The Whale* by Tre Tryckare, Cagner & Co., Sweden, and Simon & Schuster, United States, whose chief editor, Dr. Leonard Harrison Mathews, F.R.S., of the London Zoological Society, correlated material contributions from many internationally known experts on whales and whaling; *The Year of the Whale* by Victor B. Scheffer; *The Marine Mammals of the North-Western Coast of North America* by Charles M. Scammon; *Whales, Dolphins and Porpoises* published by the University of California Press and edited by Kenneth S. Norris, a collation of cetology papers presented in 1963 before the First International Symposium on Cetacean Research in Washington D.C.; and sundry findings made available by the Sandy Hook, N.J., Marine Laboratory, now a research adjunct of the Department of Commerce: and *The Blue Whale* by George L. Small. All distortions of fact for the sake of the fiction are the author's.

Also *An Introduction to Oceanography* by Cuchlaine A. M. King, University of Nottingham; *Study Guide to Oceanography* by John G. Weihaupt, chairman, physical and biological sciences, Armed Forces Institute; L. Engel *The Sea*, Life's Nature Library.

Follow
the
Whales

1

They were sunning on a patch of sand beside one of the food inlets which ran from the open sea into Jewel Bay in what had once been Baja, California, before the old nuclear wars had gouged the ancient peninsula into a chain of islands.

At least, two of them were. Two were otherwise engaged.

"Why did you bite my foot?" asked Genright. "Or should I say, why are you still nipping it?"

"Not your foot, your big toe," answered Toby Lee. "And because it is not nice to shove your foot into a lady's face, and I am a lady. I intend to bite it right off."

"What would you do if you weren't a lady?" asked the muffled voice of Tuktu Barnes, his face hidden in the crook of his arm as he lay on his belly.

"I would bite off a whole leg and plant it as a roost for the gulls," said Toby, sitting up and throwing Genright's intruding foot in the general direction of away.

"Would you water it faithfully and hope it grew leaves?" grunted Tuktu.

"Better you should soak your heads and try to figure why we are here at Baja Base, unassigned, and loafing—which can't please Commander Tod Torrance and his executive officer, Commander Jiggs Jensen, too much," Kim Rockwell said quietly. "But here we are right out of Rover School at Olympia Base, which does not usually accept Sea Wardens Third and a Sea Warden Second for rover training. If we had come to work, we'd be down in the bay herding sharks as we did before, not lolling about biting toes."

They sat up and looked at him.

Sea Warden, Second Class, and a rank grade ahead of the others owing to meritorious service, Kim was tall and wire-muscled, with a deep rib cage beneath a wide span of shoulders, and his new tan held a sun flush which would deepen into the color of pale tea. His ash-blond hair tossed in the breeze from the sea, and his eyes were green as the young combers curving to the west.

He was seventeen, young for his rank, young for the responsibilities which went with it. Yet it seemed forever since he had been screened by the Career Board for Underwater Cadet and Warden Training and accepted for in-sea duties in the Marine Service by the International Marine Council. He had worked hard ever since he left the Municipal Nursery, where all children were graded for their future places in society. He had studied the sciences of the sea eight hours a day for more than ten years before his first assignment. To advance his knowledge further, even his resting hours had been turned into classroom use by the hypnosleep machines.

Kim warmed his eyes on his companions. They had been similarly trained and were also moving through the ranks of the Services as they gained experience and additional knowledge. A scrap of Service ceremony scratched at his mind: "This band of brothers . . ." And this group was particularly close, almost a telepathic unit, made so by shared danger, shared enthusiasm, shared in-sea daily work.

The Service held many such units. The Service was a brotherhood, and a vital one. What remained of civilization—the great hive cities burrowed deep in North and South America, Asia, Africa, and Europe since the nuclear wars altered the continents and changed the more than 80 per cent of the world now covered with water—depended upon those who worked the shores, the continental slopes, and the depths. The sea range was the world's warehouse, which held the resources for mankind's survival until all earth would once again be healed.

"Why are you looking at me as though I were not here?" asked Genright, staring at Kim.

"Maybe you aren't here," drawled Tuktu. "To me you are very wispy, practically a shadow."

"You only say that because I'm black."

"You see, black shadows are very hard on wispy black people," added Tuktu.

"I got a white arm to replace the one the giant squid ate off that time in the kelp forest."

"That's how I know you're here," murmured Tuktu blandly.

"If Toby Lee bites off my toe, maybe I could get a white one for it," speculated Genright.

"They might not have your size," giggled Toby.

"They might have a used finger or so that would do," contributed Tuktu.

"What would I use it for down there?" mused Genright.

"Surprise scratching," laughed Kim. "But just keep it up, you clowns. Anything to avoid thinking. You'll come to it though, sooner or later. The question is, What are we doing at Baja loafing?"

"We are waiting for new orders," said Tuktu thoughtfully, his eyes squinched, and he nodded as if to confirm his own words, relaxed as a sackful of wet seaweed. He was wide and stocky, with a deep chest that seemed to extend to his waistline under an umbrella of vast shoulders.

Tuktu came from the North, from the McKinley City hive deep within the remaining mountain ranges of what had once been Alaska. He had served his apprenticeship in the Bering Sea before beginning his transfer to other duties. Generations ago Tuktu's ancestors had been Eskimos wresting their own hard harvest from the sea to survive. It wasn't odd that he hoped to be a specialist in nutrients someday, a scholar in the foods of ocean plants, mammals, fishes, and other sea-spawned life forms.

Genright Selsor, who had been Tuktu's in-sea patrol partner during most of their warden service, was totally unlike him physically. Genright was built like a jointed sea eel, and he moved like a wand in wind with superb co-ordination. His skin was velvet and black as the great deeps. Against it his right arm looked like a white exclamation mark, and he was lucky to have it. The Service doctors, using the body regeneration stocks, had taken what was available to save his life after the battle with a giant squid in the kelp jungle.

Genright had been schooled in the mighty burrow city which lay deep, safe, and busy under the plateau of ancient Ethiopia, and one day he might be one of the ranking oceanographic chemists.

"I agree that we are waiting for orders, but if we were waiting for ordinary orders, don't you think Commander Torrance would have given them to us when we arrived? We've been doodling around here a week now."

"These must be special orders," said Genright.

"Right," said Kim, "but why?"

"Because I, for one, am very special," muttered Tuktu.

"I am, without doubt, much more special," added Genright.

Toby Lee tossed her head, waved an airy nothing to the sky with a languid hand, and managed to give the impression that she had arched her slim back. "Hum ho and ho hum," she said.

Kim's green eyes sparkled, turned a dark emerald, and a small quirk tilted the corners of his mouth. "I see no contest," he said softly.

Toby Lee was most special to him. She was doll-high, with a face like a flower and an all-girl form, and she had shared a silicate habitat bubble on the sea bed with him for months of patrol duty in the kelp forests. She had been his working twin in the shark pens. They had shared the amazing mission set by the Council of Cities in the search for a long-vanished hive and the startling secret it held. She was part of him, walking uninvited into his thoughts with wit and insight through some warm process as simple as breathing.

The mind-bending psykes of the International Marine Council were resolute in the manner in which they conditioned members of the Warden Service for in-sea duty. Nobody could ever say they never failed completely. But some relationships did not work out as predicted.

Kim watched the play of sunlight on her golden skin. If the history tapes and computer archives of the hive cities were right, the nation of her heritage had produced fishery and sea farm experts for a thousand years. Her forebears had taken 90 per cent of their protein from the sea. Her historic homeland had long disappeared, but the old maps still held the name Japan.

Toby Lee was a year older than Kim, but he now ranked her a full grade in the Service. However, time could close that gap. He never doubted her competency, her skills, or her ability to carry more than her share of the work load. That slim, agile, female body held an amazing strength. Her affinity with the sea was total.

Genright and Tuktu twisted to their feet. They brushed sand from the scraps of sargassum cloth wisps that served them as beach garb.

"We are going swimming," announced Tuktu. "For fun and for free. It won't cost the government a cent. We want to make this contribution of our own time generously. When we come back we'll tell you why we seem to be in exile waiting for special orders."

"Thanks," said Kim. "I think I already know."

"So do I," added Toby Lee.

"Don't you want us to go swimming?" asked Genright blandly. "They don't want us to go swimming, Tuktu."

"I don't care whether or not you swim or not," grunted Kim.

"Okay, order us to go swimming then. You rank us. Say 'Barnes and Selsor, you are hereby ordered to go swimming.' And specify the ocean, not that food canal or any buckets you might have hidden around."

"How about drinking cups?" said Tuktu.

"No drinking cups either."

Toby Lee sprang to her feet, but Genright and Tuktu were already loping toward the beach, a breeze-tossed confetti of laughter echoing behind them. Kim heaved himself erect beside her. He squinted into the glare bouncing off the foaming surf line, automatically and expertly examining the water. He noted that Genright and Tuktu had halted at the water's edge and were also checking the sea. Long training made good habits, and good habits often as not meant survival to those who worked in the waters. Out there somewhere, thought Kim, dolphins were chousing food fish toward the inlet canals of Jewel Bay to become meals for thousands of herd sharks, who would in turn become meals and medicines for the hive cities. Out there, in the depths, sonic emitters were aiding the dolphins, and maybe a few wardens, piping small school fish onward through the ocean abutting the canals. And nobody ever knew for sure exactly what bigger life forms might be following the smaller ones except that if there were bigger creatures about, they would own appetites to match their sizes.

The surf was orderly, and the green combers wearing foam-white shakos marched in straight files. A steady west wind had given them some dimension, however, and they seemed to be six to eight feet at the curl.

Genright and Tuku vanished beneath one of the ranks and emerged into the smooth sea beyond.

"They are too much," said Toby softly, smiling like a mother.

Kim grinned. "They don't let their smarts ruin their fun, that's for sure."

They walked into the water and stood thigh-high in suds, hooking their toes into the firm white sand footing and balancing unconsciously against the backwash. Kim licked a spray splash from his cheek. "High saline content," he said. "Very gluey, plastic waves, almost perfect for surfing."

Toby Lee giggled. "You might take a look at the perfect surfers too."

A scant quarter of a mile from them Genright's head peered from a green wall of humping water with Tuktu's grinning brown face immediately above it. There was a tumult of flashing arms at the curl, then Genright's slim black body, arms outstretched, stiffened into a human surfboard. Simultaneously Tuktu seemed to eject from the sea, rise to his feet, and remain frozen in precarious balance. As nearly as the watchers could tell, Tuktu had one foot on Genright's rump and the other in the middle of his back. Together they whizzed down the slope of sea immediately ahead of the curl, body surfer and rider, until the wave crested. They parted and peeled off into the side of the wave before it collapsed under its own weight. They picked themselves up in the shallows and sloshed toward Toby Lee and Kim in the wash.

"You like my tame surfboard?" asked Tuktu.

"He's a better one," said Genright. "He's wider, and you can jump up and down on him without slipping off."

"You've been practicing, that's for sure," said Kim. "And you can teach Toby and me. That looks like real fun."

"You think Toby Lee can carry three?" asked Genright. "Lie down on your face, Toby. We'll tromple over you for size. Might as well find out now if you bend in the middle or not."

"I'll bend you in the middle, you big slab."

"What would you do if you weren't a lady?" asked Tuktu.

"Hammer him down until he'd be up to his neck in an inch of water," she said firmly.

"That's nice," Genright murmured absently. "Incidentally, Kim, that surfing thing isn't a bad trick to learn. Got us out of some trouble once. We were pretty new in the kelp forest and working close to shore in gill suits one day when a real tricky jet current banged Tuktu against a sawtoothed rock. Nicked an artery in his leg. I don't remember how we thought of it, but we caught a wave, with Tuktu hanging on my back, for a quick ride to shore, where we got a tourniquet on the leg."

"You thought of it," said Tuktu. "You are a hero. You saved my life."

"You bled all over me."

"All reeky and gruesome and messy and disgusting?"

"Ukk!" said Toby.

"Anyhow, we've practiced a lot of funnies in the surf since," added Genright, "and it's nice and crazy to do too."

The four of them strolled up the beach and headed slowly toward the canal bank. The sun was beginning to slide down the afternoon slope of the sky although Kim could still feel its reminding sting on his back, which itched as the salt dried.

"You said you'd tell us why we were sitting around Baja waiting for special orders," he said. "Or did the two of you forget while you were swimming?"

"You and Toby said you knew," grunted Tuktu.

"All right," said Genright. "When I count to three everybody tells. One, two . . . what comes after two?"

"Two what?" asked Tuktu.

"One angry me," said Kim, an edge in his voice.

"Okay, okay," hastened Genright. "The only reason we can think of that might mean special orders for all four of us is in the sea babies."

"Or something to do with them, certainly," said Toby Lee softly.

"Right," interrupted Kim. "And either Commanders Torrance and Jensen don't know what our orders will be, or they have been asked to wait until someone arrives to give us special briefing. What's more, I have a very clear idea of just who that person will be."

"Oh, no," muttered Tuktu.

"Oh, no," echoed Genright.

"Oh, yes," said Toby Lee. "Commander Brent, or whatever his title is."

"Or whatever he does," speculated Tuktu.

"And not to me, I hope," said Genright.

"Or the sea babies either," Toby Lee's voice was crisp.

"As I remember, Commander Brent once wanted the sea babies destroyed," Tuktu muttered somberly.

They still moved through the sand toward the canal bank, but mechanically now. They were all remembering. They remembered the Cryo, that strange violet-eyed man shocked back to knowledge of a forgotten hive city by a lightning bolt here at Baja Base. The Cryo was one of the Long Sleepers which sometimes appeared from the recesses of the once bomb-battered world. Their name came from the science called "cryogenic interment." It was a deep-freeze halt of all bodily functions complete with total preservation of all physical organs and cybernetic maintenance of all cell structures.

The Cryos were stockpiled humanity placed away by governments able to foresee the onrushing destruction of earth but unable to halt it. Most of them were geniuses: great healers, biologists, mathematicians, metallurgists, legal philosophers, artists. They were men and women who might be able to build the future environments for the remnants of mankind who had survived the nuclear wars. Many were young, many worn with fatal illnesses which might be cured by the sciences of the future.

It was the Cryo Ury Kaane, now dead, who had led them to the lost Hive Hawaii, where forgotten masters of chemical genesis, creators of so-called artificial life, had made a new form of mankind, a thinking man-creature designed for the sea and adapted to life in the oceans should the dwellers of the dry earth completely vanish.

It was assumed that the life masters of the lost burrow city had worked for centuries on the project while still racing time to keep some strain of man alive. But they were not the real pioneers.

Long before them, and long before the rending of the earth while there was still a United Nations and even separate countries with their own governments, there had been work in evolutionary control.

School children as far back in history as the twentieth century, the same period in history which saw the atom unchained for the first time, knew about DNA and RNA. They knew that DNA, or deoxyribonucleic acid, set the main patterns in all human heredity, and that RNA, or ribonucleic acid, was the message-carrying chemical that told the life cells how best to form the patterns set by DNA. More, they knew that man, using DNA and RNA, were coming close to the creation of artificial life, even in human beings, that would not show any differences from natural life.

It seemed logical that a scientific laboratory could be somebody's "mother." And after the years of emergencies and crises that finally saw most of earth explode, laboratory babies became as commonplace as naturally born ones, maybe much better ones in a world that was forced into rigid disciplines for survival.

But with more than 80 per cent of the world covered by water, it was the lost Hawaii hive city that realized that some form of man had to be created for life in the sea itself.

It was hardly a new idea. Nature held it first millions of years before any men existed. Many of her evolutionary creatures had started as land animals and returned to the oceans of their forebears; the whales, for instance, the dolphins—all the air breathers redesigned within fusiform or torpedo-shaped bodies which could move in the density of water and give their owners life.

And now there were real mermen and mermaids somewhere in the great sea ranges. Sea babies! Kim, Toby Lee, Genright, and Tuktu had seen the last hatch from the destroyed Hawaii burrow city born during the dramatic missions known as Hawaii Search.

"Don't look now," said Genright. "But somebody is standing where we were lying before Kim ordered us to go swimming."

"I am not really looking," muttered Tuktu. "It seems to be three bodies, not one body."

"They are all somebodies, and all our bosses," grunted Kim.

"And one of them is friendly, lovable, joyful Commander Brent," added Toby Lee.

"But why Commanders Torrance and Jensen as well?" wondered Genright. "All they had to do was blow a whistle and we'd have zinged right up to the office."

"Would you believe no whistles?" asked Tuktu.

"No," said Kim thoughtfully, "but I'd believe that we are going to get our orders right out here in the beautiful sunshine where none of the little wardens running around the base will ever know we ever had a meeting with this much brass at all."

"How can I hear orders when I'm out of uniform?" asked Genright.

"Well, they trip you. Two of them hold you down. The other one hollers in your ear," said Tuktu.

"Wrong," said Toby. "All wrong. Commander

Brent will tell us that we're out of uniform, and he'll do it so you think you are in uniform. Then you'll hear orders or anything else just as if you were standing at attention."

"Toby's got it absolutely right," said Kim. "But uniform or bare as we could get, I'd suggest we salute."

"I can get barer than this," Toby said darkly.

"Then they'd all salute first," said Kim, flashing one of his rare, wide grins. "But not ahead of me."

"I don't care about a thing now," said Toby. "My whole year is made."

They moved briskly, out of the sand, through a skirting of grasses, and climbed the embankment to the canal side. They approached the three waiting men, snapped to attention, and saluted.

"Sirs," they said.

"You are out of uniform," said Commander Brent, his gray-green eyes probing, "but we appreciate Service courtesy." He returned their salute meticulously.

Commander Brent, or sometimes civilian Mr. Brent, was not a tall man, although the width of his shoulder span seemed designed for a man of lengthier inches. He stood tall, and the air of quiet authority and competent confidence about him indicated that he was a man too big to be gauged by physical measurements. When the young wardens before him had seen him last he was in command of Mission Hawaii Search, and as the direct representative of the all-powerful Council of Cities. His voice was soft, although the wardens had heard it snap with the cold, claw tones of demand actions.

"Stand easy," he said, and then with even softer tones, he asked, "Figured it out yet?"

"Yes, sir," said Kim. "The sea babies plus the Rover School plus this sort of rest and recreation period which we assumed would mean special orders."

Commander Tod Torrance nodded approvingly.

He was a spare man, slat-lean and wiry with some thirty years in the Service. His hair was gray, with the dull sheen of arctic ice on a cloudy day. Years of squinting in sea glare and peering subocean shadows had arranged tiny nests of wrinkles at the corners of his hazel eyes.

"Bright, very bright," he added. "But then you disappointed Commander Jensen. He thought you might come asking about your status at Headquarters."

"But only for about ten seconds," rumbled Jensen. "Then I remembered both your ages and the teachings of the elders. Don't ask because you might be told, and never volunteer because you might be accepted. Further, as I recall, the Service teaches the art of waiting very early and very well."

Somewhere in his huge mid-section there was a subdued explosion that might have been a chuckle. Commander Jiggs Jensen was a bear of a man with a passion for getting jobs done right, but all who ever served with him or under him knew him for a truly gentle giant. He and Torrance had worked as in-sea buddies for decades, and upward from the sea ranges to onshore command posts.

The three officials were in spotless green Service uniforms, and the Baja sun was hot. Commander Brent narrowed his eyes at a trio of terns about to make a swoop over his shoulder to snack at the food inlet. He gave the impression that he did not care for any good turns done from a tern's point of view. They were messy birds.

"This is hardly a social call," he snapped. "Ordinarily I do not conduct beachhead meetings. On the other hand, I thought it best not to give anyone reason to wonder why three high-ranking members of this Service bothered to consult with four minor wardens."

Kim felt a smile form in his head and sensed that Toby shared it. He carefully suppressed any facial expression.

"Whatever is said here is secret information just as Mission Hawaii Search was, and that is highly classified. Its details are known only to the Council of Cities and the Service people who conducted it."

Commander Brent paused.

"I would have been here a week ago had I been able to resolve other considerations in connection with your new orders. Further, I wished to consult with your instructors at Olympia Rover School.

"You did well there. I expected it. I might say I took it for granted."

He allowed himself a certain warming about the eyes.

"Did you notice anything unusual about your rover training? Speak up."

There was a brief silence as the young wardens allowed Kim to assume their mutually granted leadership.

"Sir," said Kim. "I don't think any of us could give you an honest answer. None of us had ever been through formal rover training. Emphasis on sea survival techniques we expected. The classes on new equipment, weaponry, and underwater mapping processes didn't seem surprising."

He hesitated and glanced around at his companions.

"It did seem that we were getting an awful lot of sound detection, sub-sea sound analysis, and echo-location hours, however. And we felt that we were getting more studies in whale biology, whale migratory patterns, whale history . . . just whales of time on whales, sir, than we expected."

"Good," snapped Commander Brent. "You did notice. The extra studies in cetology are unusual in most rover courses. But then you are going to be whalers in a most unusual fashion."

2

There was a boil in the canal below them. A sleek black back arched out of the water, and a big triangular dorsal fin seemed to point an admonitory finger. There was a snorting blast of spray. And a fifteen-foot dolphin from the open sea startled a school of foot-long pilchards toward a hastier destiny in the waiting reaches of the bay, where the forever-hungry shark herds cruised.

"The snort sounded like a form of criticism," mumbled Commander Jensen, his face cracked in a grin. "That particular member of the whale family must think you're all too puny for messing with the big cousins."

"I am inclined to agree with him," whispered Genright.

"Come, come," said Commander Brent. "Any questions?"

"Sir," said Toby Lee. "What happened to our sea babies?"

"First, they were not your sea babies," snapped Commander Brent. "Second, they died. And despite every effort to keep them alive and well, they died naturally, although considering the circumstances, it is hard to say just what in their case was natural."

He locked the four wardens together with a single cold stare.

"We think they were mistakes," he said.

"With all due respect, sir," said Kim, "they were still a form of mankind."

"And with your respect noted, young man, we, meaning the best scientists of the burrow cities, think now that they were not the *only* such form created by the great laboratory geneticists of the lost Hawaii hive. They were merely the *last* such attempt to create a man with a sea form to live and survive without contact with a poisoned land.

"You will recall that when we discovered them"—he nodded to Toby Lee—"that there was speculation to the effect that at least two other life hatches had preceded them."

The young wardens bobbed their heads in agreement.

"The best scientific assumption is now that they might have had a better chance of survival and adaptation than the sea babies. Almost certainly, they were mammals with certain alterations for life in salt water.

"Careful examination of the sea babies after they had died, with what was learned from them before their death, proved that they were a combination of both fish—the bony fishes—and mammals. Our geneticists believe that such a combination was too forced to be successful."

"May I ask a question, sir?" asked Kim.

"Do," said Commander Brent.

"Were the sea babies intelligent?"

"Do you mean did they have human intelligence?"

"Yes, sir."

"As you pointed out yourself, they were a form of mankind. Although, as you know, we only had two of the young, male and female, to observe, we think their problem was physical and physical only. Certainly they were well . . . oh, so very well . . . cared for. . . ."

It might have been a scrap of cloud wisping past the sun, but Kim thought he saw a faint shadow darken the Commander's face before he continued, a tiny tint of hurt.

"But we don't know much of anything for sure. If the offspring we saw as your sea babies failed in the oceans, did the first or second adaptations succeed? If so, where are they? What are they thinking and doing? Are they upsetting the food supplies the cities depend upon? Are they a menace to those who live on land?

"The questions are endless, and our answers are guesses."

Commander Torrance interrupted.

"But the Service has a basic operating assumption," he said, "and we're going to go with it."

"He means that there is now a theory which seems believable enough to spend money and risk lives, mostly young." Commander Jiggs Jensen spoke bluntly and cheerfully.

"That's nice," grunted Tuktu.

Kim watched Commander Brent's shoulders stiffen. Commander Brent was a man who preferred discipline in a straight line. He was a man who did not always consider levity to be a laughing matter. And he was obviously a man with a serious problem.

"That's enough," he said, and his voice was chilled. "It is believed that *all* of the human prototypes which came from the laboratories of the lost hive city in a sea-adapted form were released into the ocean habitat. The first creation may have survived, but it is dubious. The second, a greatly refined version of the first, may right now be living and propagating. The third, your sea babies—we don't think so.

"In any case, we are going to make a search for all versions. We are going to concentrate our efforts on the so-called *second* birthing. That's the one we think produced the improved mammal merman. In fact, our geneticists say he may outwardly resemble the dolphins a great deal. He will almost certainly share some characteristics, both physical and biological, with most mammalian forms of sea life.

"We assume that if he is prospering with the advantages of superior intelligence and the ability to think, that he may already be able to control, live among, and use the other mammals."

"And so, sir," said Kim, "we follow the whales."

Commander Brent nodded. "You have the heart for it."

Kim shook his head slowly as though he were lost in some thought which seemed unthinkable, and as he did so, he felt the warm, questing touch of Toby Lee's mind in his own.

"What, sir, do we do if and when we find our cousins?" she asked.

Commander Brent exhaled deeply.

"I am not going to mince words with any of you," he said. "The answer is that I do not know their ultimate fate. The Council of Cities is still confronting the fact that there may be two types of mankind now sharing this planet. I do know that you will make your reports, attempt to locate whatever passes for home bases among these strangers, and supply all possible data concerning them.

"The truth is that you may never see any of them after years of search."

"Years of search?" asked Tuktu, suddenly startled.

"A figure of speech," Commander Jiggs Jensen said comfortingly.

"Us whales got lots of time," muttered Genright.

Commander Brent permitted himself the sound of breaking sticks, which he considered a chuckle.

"That's the essence of the matter for now," he said. "You will report in uniform and for duty to Commander Torrance's office at base following the sundown meal. Details of your orders will be discussed at that time. Before then you will have a chance to talk this over among yourselves and formulate as many questions as you deem necessary. Dismissed."

He picked up the other two officers with his eyes, and together they walked off along the embankment toward the headquarters compound.

"Order us to go swimming again," said Tuktu.

"And order us not to come back," added Genright.

"I don't believe my sea babies died a natural death," snapped Toby Lee.

"You mean they were fried and eaten like mackerel?" asked Genright eagerly.

"You are disgusting."

"Too true, too true," moaned Tuktu. "He is a burden."

"Do you realize just what we are going to be part of?" asked Kim. "Come on now. I want all the good brains going for a change."

"A search that may take years," said Genright.

"Where were you going otherwise?" asked Tuktu. "But that's not what Kim is concerned about. Not really. What he means is that, like it or not, we are going to be in the middle of a very important Council of Cities decision. Not that we're so much. Who needs four teeny wardens?"

"Me," said Genright. "I need me especially."

"If we should be lucky enough to find the new sea people, or even if we don't, our information and our reports will reach high places," continued Tuktu, undisturbed. "And if we should ever make contact—or be able to communicate—then we might actually say whether or not these, ahh, ughh, strangers would be allowed to exist.

"I haven't forgotten that the first orders back there in that lost hive city were to destroy the sea babies."

"But they decided not to, you know," said Toby Lee. "People don't destroy people."

"Back to the archives and the history tapes for you, my girl," said Genright. "Some few thousand years ago, give or take a week maybe because I'm not very good at history, people not only destroyed people, they destroyed the world people lived on as well. Now these people we're talking about won't even look like people, and some people will say they're not and call them an oceanic resource.

"Do I make myself clear?"

"Unclearly, but yes," said Toby Lee.

"Genright's right," Kim said seriously. "Especially when he mentions oceanic resources. The needs of the cities come first. Figure it out. Commander Brent talked about us as whalers, special whalers. Then he talked about the possibility of the new people controlling other sea mammals and using them. Notice I said 'using them.'

"The supply administrations of the hives would call it depleting the herds, the herds that the Service has spent hundreds and hundreds of years reviving to feed and supply the cities."

Tuktu scratched himself inelegantly.

"I'm thinking of what whales mean to the cities," he said. "There's the oil. Not that we need it for light and heat or energy. The A power takes care of that. But the wars vaporized the petroleum man once used, and the hydroponic operators and laboratory geniuses can't produce enough vegetable oils. So there's the whale oil for diet fats, for soaps, and for glycerin, which, in turn, is used for medical and industrial reasons. And then there's oil again for varnishes and inks—"

Toby Lee interrupted.

"And don't forget the sperm oils and spermaceti, which are really liquid waxes for lubricants, detergents, dyes, bleaches, alcohols," she said.

"And the meats," said Genright, "fresh, frozen, dried, smoked, and very good for you, according to the instructor at Rover School, because of its high content of histidine—"

"I know. I know," yelled Tuktu. "Without histidine everybody would be two inches high because without it you can't grow. And how about blood powder and bone powder for the nitrogens needed to grow things in the green houses? And the gelatins richer than those we get from the kelp stipes for food and even photographic film? And ambergris for scents? And hides for leathers?"

"So, we all did our homework," said Kim. "And while we're thinking of what the whales mean to the cities, add vitamin A from their livers and insulin to help people sick with diabetes. Count in what our instructors said about ACTH, the adrenocorticotrophic hormone, to treat arthritis. Think of all the uses for bones—"

Toby Lee shrieked.

"What's that for?" asked Genright.

"Simply attention," she said quietly. "And to remind you that if the sea people do not view whales as a quick lunch, for instance, they are still people."

"That may well be the trouble," said Kim. "Time to go."

They reported to Commander Torrance's headquarters office trim in Service greens with short-sleeved, bloused uniform shirts and shorts, their shark leather ankle boots gleaming. The amber dusk about them was soft, and to the west the sea was saffron not yet blooded by the plunging sun.

They found Commanders Torrance and Jiggs Jensen hunched over a long, flat, map-covered table waiting for them. Commander Brent was not there.

"He took the freight rocket back to the Denver hive," explained Commander Jensen. "One more meeting connected with your assignment, and apparently half the entire Service's as well. Said he'd see you at sea if necessary. We'll handle the briefing. That'll please you, won't it?" His smile was warm. "But enjoy now, pay later."

"Step around here and look at this map," said Commander Torrance. "It's an antique, but like so many things stowed away when humanity decided to commit suicide, it's fairly valid."

"This is a map made by oceanographic biologists maybe a thousand years ago. It shows the migratory routes of the animal once called the California gray whale. The California is gone, but the gray whale endures. You've seen them when you worked in the kelp forests.

"The gray has changed some, naturally, due, we think, to radiation and general oceanic alterations from the old wars. They are still baleen whales filtering small marine organisms through their baleen sieves for food.

"They are still lung breathers, and they still surface to breathe. But their size has changed owing to mutation factors. The grays that used these old routes weighed in at approximately thirty-five tons, according to the study reports of that day. They cruised about four knots an hour, could sustain speeds up to ten knots for maybe two hours at a time, and could achieve up to thirty knots when they decided to heave out of the water in breaching."

He paused.

"But you know all this, I'm sure, and it's fresh to you. However, the point that I'm making is to expand all the old figures for today's grays, or any other whales.

"However, back to the map. You'll notice that they were travelers like all the big cetaceans. They roamed from right here at Baja, before the changes, up the coast of what was the United States and Canada, zinged west to the old Aleutian Islands into the Bering Sea and along the coasts of Siberia and the Kamchatka Peninsula. They went into the Arctic Ocean as well, right to the fringes of the pack ice.

"That was their summer journey. In the winter

they came south again to mate and bear young, mostly in the bays and coves of Baja."

"About nine to ten thousand miles round trip," said Commander Jensen. "You may get used to it. You are joining the gray pods."

"But you'll run into blue whales that will give you something to see, about a hundred and fifty feet and two hundred and fifty tons of something," added Commander Torrance. "And of course the sperms, the great toothed creatures, which feed on whatever is around—"

"I resign," muttered Genright.

"For both of us," said Tuktu.

"I know you want the big fact as far as you are personally concerned. You'll remain as in-sea buddies just as you were in the kelp forest and here in the shark pens. But there won't be any break every three months to get away from each other. Just remember the rover regulations for teams or small units. Anything done for the cause of compatibility is not only condoned but required."

"Just don't try keeping white mice for pets," Commander Jensen said, laughing.

"That means Kim and Toby as a unit, and Genright and Tuktu as another," continued Commander Torrance.

"As to equipment, each team of you will have one of the new pelagic work subs."

He paused.

"All I can say is that Commander Brent must think highly of your capabilities," he said. "These subs are the latest in the Service, and there are only fifteen in the entire fleet. You remember the *Polaris*, in which you served during Hawaii Search? These are thirty-foot versions of her. Radial filament, weldglass pressure hull tested to more than 250,000 pounds per square inch. Nuclear-powered all the way with in-hull sea engines with induction coils driving her on water jets. Even the anti-gravity keel."

He noted the puzzle lines that furrowed Toby Lee's brow.

"Explain, Rockwell," he said.

"Well, sir, as Commander Cassius of the *Polaris* cleared it for me, the keel's made of one of the new stabilized metals with an amazing property of changing molecular densities when we apply energy. Its mass stays the same, but its weight can be changed in any section along its length at any time. Its total weight can be altered enough to take us to the bottom at about any depth. It can change the total boat weight so we can hover, hold at any depth, or surface quickly. The boat does not need propulsion to keep it at depth."

"Very good, Rockwell," said Commander Torrance. He gazed at Toby Lee. "You were all checked out with this craft at Rover School. You all had operating instructions on the boat, I assume?"

"Yes sir," said Toby Lee. "I just forgot for a minute about the keel. We did get a week of sea tests as operators."

"And we certainly had plenty of time on the boat's fully controlled environmental systems, all the acoustical and vision devices, all the recorders, sensors, and biological snoopers too," Tuktu put in. "They're really beautiful."

"We also used the in-hull pressure bubbles for any depth exits and entrances with all types of diving and swimming equipment," said Genright.

"And of course we got pretty handy with the navigational and control systems," said Kim. "But I must say, sir, I never thought we'd catch one of our own for quite a few years. Well, not until we'd worked our way to regular rover rank."

"You have," snapped Commander Torrance. "At least as far as Commander Brent is concerned. How many of the open-range men have ever seen sea babies or worked with a Cryo?"

"Sir, none of us have ever had any real experience with whales either," said Genright.

"You are not instructed to assume any of the duties of the regular pelagic herdsmen," Commander Torrance informed him. "As a matter of fact, you will stay away from milking operations, plankton seedings, slaughter croppings, breeding operations as *direct* orders.

"You may be asked to assist the regular rover herdsmen from time to time as special help is needed. But probably one of the major reasons you have been selected for your assignment is that you lack experience with whales, and that whatever you see and record may have a significance that older and wiser pelagic experts might miss simply because they have seen so much for so long.

"Does that make sense to you?"

"Yes, sir," said Kim thoughtfully. "It does when you add it to the fact that we, at least, have some idea of what we may be seeking."

"And no one else presently doing *normal* Service work does. Remember that always," added Commander Torrance. "You will be given special communication links for your reports. As I get it, there will be special mother vehicles in various parts of the range to serve as reporting centers. The *Polaris* under Commander Cassius, whom you know, will be one of them."

"Why were we assigned to the gray whales, sir?" asked Tuktu. "I mean, why the grays specifically?"

"Rockwell, answer him," said Commander Torrance.

Kim thought a moment, his green eyes turning darker.

Jiggs Jensen prompted him. "You saw their migratory routes."

In his mind's eye, Kim saw something else.

He saw a golden cavern in the heart of a water-buried mountain, its sides banked with strange clicking machines with thousands of swimming forms milling in the mysterious amniotic liquid it contained.

He saw the sea babies, some two feet in length, their backs green-blue from head to tail, a tail which looked like a caudal juncture of two ankles with the feet turned into a fluke. They resembled scrambled dolphins with less-humped backs flaunting a feathery plume of dorsal fin. And where the pectoral fins should have been straight and rigid, theirs were webbed and showed clearly a set of usable fingers and a thumb—baby hands adapted for the sea.

And he saw their eyes, round, lidless, and violet in hue, shining with a blaze of awareness.

Then he saw the open sea in the dawn sun with the small forms bobbing and their dorsal plumes erect and waving. And he saw the hatch swim away as a giant school.

"Of course," he said. "The sea babies headed north and east from the old charts which marked Hawaii toward the Aleutians, as shown on this map of the gray whale routes. The old Aleutians, the Bering Sea, and the northeastern Pacific itself are home to the grays. At least, home base," he amended. "So we observe the grays. Am I right, sir?"

"Who knows?" Commander Torrance shrugged. "But it's the same assumption the biologists made for starters."

"You know, of course, that the business of observation is not limited to peeking out of peepholes at the pretty ocean." Commander Jensen was grinning, and he patted a thick, bound volume of papers on the map table.

"These instruction manuals call for about ten hours a day of pure, wonderful drudgery for you all. Everything from water samplings to exercise periods, from underwater mapping to nutrient analysis—busy, busy, busy hands, as we say in the Service.

"Now for the cookie break and then more story hour," he added.

There was never a Marine Service corps in the history of man without some hot pot brewing on its premises. Commander Jensen produced mugs, slabs of algae-dough bread pocked with hydrogarden berries, and steaming seaweed tea.

They talked. Shoptalk. About the whale herdsmen who spent their lives with the herds, about the explorer rovers who wandered remote regions of the open sea ranges years at a time poking into anything at all which might be of use to the cities: currents, tides, strange life forms, odd geographic facts about the sort of people who made up the Service itself.

"We're the last of the free," murmured Genright.

There was an odd silence.

"What made you say that, Genright?" Commander Torrance asked softly.

"No rank, sir?" Kim queried him hastily.

"In this room only," said Commander Jensen, "and that very carefully."

Genright was careful. "Well," he said. "The psykes pick types at birth, and more than half the births are controlled. When there is little physical living room for people anywhere on earth, and limited food to feed them, then the people within that living space have to be selected according to function and disciplined down to their deepest breath. Further, they have to be conditioned, as we have been, to accept their own part in a society which has to eliminate any possible human friction or conflict to exist. We were typed at birth for Service duty. Just had to be, you know. Because somewhere in our genes were human characteristics that couldn't be controlled for hive living no matter how much conditioning we got. So the city fathers stamped our rumps for seagoing and put us to work. But I have no doubt at all that if the Service weren't necessary to city survival—human survival, that is—we'd have been discarded just as coldly as . . . as *kerplop*."

"*Kerplop?*" asked Tuktu.

"And that's not all," Genright continued serenely. "They take a look at a mess of genes that may turn into some fella who's going to ask a lot of questions, like who's got the right to lean on who and is there a better way to do things, and he has to go. That is, if human beings are going to make it as a species. So send the potential troublemakers to sea, where they can serve the race until there's enough world restored to let everybody ramble. That's what I meant. We're the last of the free."

"You wouldn't be advising a change in the system, would you, Genright?" asked Commander Torrance coldly.

"No, sir," said Genright. "It could probably be

improved, but without it, and those who planned it and made it work from the beginning, there wouldn't be a human race on earth."

"You might give the system credit for that freedom you're talking about too," interruped Kim.

"Say," said Toby Lee.

Kim grinned. "Well, it seems to me that the planners knew it would take certain types to work in the oceans and make them productive. Uncouth ones that needed lots of room and lots of challenge that would demand new skills and individual efforts and, maybe, sharper wits than are needed in routine city living. You know a lot of poison has gone from the earth since the wars, and someday there will be plenty of land outside the burrows.

"I'll bet the Council of Cities has a plan for just that time. And you know what? It says, get those wardens out of the oceans and turn 'em loose on land and make 'em put it in shape for the rest of us . . . trees, rocks, animals, farms, houses, churches, all the stuff in the archives saved before the wars. You know what else it says? It says the Service people have to do it, because they've had space and distances and have had to depend pretty much on themselves to do their jobs. The city people can't do it. They wouldn't know how to handle daylight. The cities did their job in saving the seed, but only our ocean types will know how to sow it again. And just because we had that freedom Genright's talking about, such as it is."

"You mean there's a plan for us to take over the works?" asked Tuktu, wide-eyed.

"I'm not saying for sure," answered Kim. "But it figures. And I'm not saying it will happen in our time. That's still a sick land outside the cities as far as we know, and the oceans aren't all that well, either. But they're all we have."

"It occurs to me that if we listened to you youngsters long enough, we might hear treason," grunted Commander Jiggs Jensen. "I might remind you, as long as rank is out during this beddy-time story hour, that some people have been more conditioned than others, and that abstract thinking outside of what they've been schooled to think makes them unhappy. Anyone of them hearing you spout off about rules, regulations, and reasons would turn you in to the authorities for recycling."

"Commander Brent once hinted that I needed it," said Kim. "I don't think he meant it."

"He didn't," said Commander Torrance with a thin smile. "If he had, you'd have been repsyched down to the bare bones, or else, *kerplop*."

"*Kerplop?*" murmured Commander Jensen.

A door slammed sharply at the end of the corridor which lead to the headquarters office from the Baja Base complex. Jensen, moving lightly and swiftly, crossed from his position at the map table, opened the office door, and peered down the hall. He looked a long moment, turned, and faced the question in their eyes.

"Wind?" His statement was a query.

"That door's on the east side of the building," Commander Torrance said softly. "Wind's from the west tonight. Bothersome. I wouldn't want anything overheard about the mission, not a peep. You all heard Brent's instructions. And come to think of it, I wouldn't want anybody to overhear all the philosophy. Half-baked or not."

"We'll look around a bit," said Commander Jensen. "Anything else? Any questions? Rockwell?"

"It's about sound," said Kim. "That door bang reminded me."

"I said we'd look into it," snapped Commander Jensen.

"I didn't mean anything about the door, sir. But earlier, when we were talking about the whale herdsmen, I meant to ask about sound as in echo location and communication from man to whales or from whales to men. Sonar ranging or what the Rover School instructors called "ketophonation" when they talked about vibrations produced by whales.

"Well, we can talk to our dolphins through our sonic warblers when we're doing in-sea work, because we know their so-called language—their sound emission code and range. They talk back to us, and we pick it up through the receiving units on our face masks or any other receivers wherever we are."

"Do the herdsmen actually communicate with their whales that way, or just what is the drill?"

Commander Torrance thought a moment.

"There are two pelagic herdsmen on Base for rest and recreation right now. I'll have them contact you tomorrow, and, if I know these lads, they'll be glad to tell you more than you want to hear about whales. Some of it might even be true.

"Dismissed."

Kim, Toby Lee, Tuktu and Genright saluted, spun, and collided in the doorway.

"Try four at a time," murmured Commander Jensen. He stared reflectively at Commander Torrance when they'd gone in a tattoo of feet down the corridor. "That's quite a group," he said. "How do you suppose they reached the same conclusions about certain things so much quicker than we did?"

"Smarter, maybe," said the top executive of Baja Base. "But they make me very homesick for my youth."

"*Kerplop*," his second-in-command said, smiling.

3

The next morning, they were in fatigues, the shapeless work clothes of the Base, noodling about one of the coquina-cement docks, occasionally throwing a line to the wardens stowing gear aboard the small work subs used in the bay. The tank divers wearing shield suits had long gone. This group of shark handlers was going out to repair the nets set to divert beef herds from cruising into the lower bay nursery pens.

"Have a nice day," said Genright to one of the workmen.

"Watch out for the ones who want to play kissie-kissie," added Tuktu.

"And don't invite anybody to lunch," said Toby Lee, smiling sweetly.

"And never bite back," added Kim. "A shark is a valuable animal. Wardens? We have wardens to spare."

The boat loaders grinned. One of them made a rude noise.

"Yeh, I hear you experts were so great down there the sardines chased you home every night," he said.

Tuktu laughed. "You're half right," he said. "There was us about a length ahead of the sardines, which were about four inches ahead of the baddies."

"Oh, well," said the boat loader. "Next year the laboratory promises to breed 'em without teeth. But," he added reflectively, "they'll have very fierce gums, no doubt."

No one ever doubted that the work in the shark pens, which included most of the two-hundred-mile stretch of Jewel Bay, was hard and dangerous. There are no domesticated sharks. The porbeagle variants, the duskies, and the herring breeds were controllable, but barely. But the pelagic varieties, the wild ones—giant whites, makos, and tigers—mutated into fantastic sizes, could never be subdued short of pitched battle with all the weapons the Service could muster.

Kim thought about their own time with the herds. He was still thinking when they were hailed by two strangers approaching them from the shore end of the dock.

They were stringy types, easy-moving men with light smiles and horizon-seeking eyes. It would have been hard to guess their ages.

"Commander Torrance asked us to look you up," said one of them. "You Rockwell, Lee, Barnes, and Selsor?"

"Right," said Tuktu.

"I'm Flake Kellog and this is Randy Deems. Base boss says you're going to make some schoolbook surveys of whales and want to know something about sonics. That right?"

"Yes, sir," said Kim. "We're assigned to the grays as of now or whenever we sail. I guess you've worked a lot with them."

"We've worked a lot with all of them," grunted Flake Kellog. "And right now I'm sick of 'em, but

I guess a half-hour out of our playtime won't hurt. But let's find some shade."

They angled off the dock to an open-ended equipment shed and sat on some baled seaweed awaiting freight-rocket shipment to medical labs of the Denver hive.

"What I really wanted to know," said Kim, "is can you communicate with whales the same way we do with our dolphins?"

"Answer is no," said Randy Deems. "We cracked the sonic codes of the dolphins twenty centuries ago or more. They were the first cetaceans we worked with, as you know, and maybe the smartest we'll ever work with, although the bigger types aren't unintelligent.

"But being cetaceans, they certainly live in a world of sound, much of it their own making. And they surely use a fine system of echo location to navigate, find food, exchange warnings—"

"And to gossip," added Flake Kellog. "You mentioned the grays," he continued. "You'll hear 'em right enough. Mostly a series of high-frequency clicks which they bounce off moving fish, shoals, sea mounts—all sorts of possible hazards. Pretty monotonous string of clicks—"

"Flake's right," interrupted Randy. "You'll get sick of hearing it . . . *click, click, click.* . . . Now we could duplicate those clicks, and we

51

have, but we don't seem to find any two-way code that we could use from us to them and them to us."

"We've heard some of the archive recordings of whale sounds," said Tuktu. "Some man way before the wars taped a humpback whale that sounded like an orchestra mixing up oboes, cornets, and bagpipes. At least, that's what it said on the info flow."

Flake nodded. "Wait until you hear a sperm whale. He clacks, and loud enough to shatter your eardrums. And there's one called the sea canary, a beluga whale, that trills."

"Commander Torrance said you'd worked here in the bay and also in the kelp forests, so you know that the ocean is a mighty noisy place," said Randy Deems. "A pod of whales doesn't exactly produce a lullaby."

Kim was thoughtful a moment.

"Then we think that the sounds made by whales are used as echo-location signals and that they communicate among themselves with them as well. Is that right?"

"Go on," said Flake curiously.

"Well, could they make sounds that we couldn't hear? Or could something else make sounds that we couldn't hear but that whales could?"

"Smart, smart," said Randy Deems. "And the answer is maybe. The big thinkers in the cities, the anatomists and the lab behavior wizards, indicate that some cetaceans are sensitive to frequencies as high as two hundred kilohertz compared to human ears with an upper hearing limit of about twenty. We've wondered about that ourselves."

"Does anything happen when you change the frequency of the sounds you beam to them? Say, when you go way up the ultrahigh range?" asked Kim.

"Nothing we know of," said Randy, "but then, we're working people, not experimenters. It's enough to do our job taking care of those monsters."

Genright jammed his elbow into Tuktu's ribs. "If you could talk to a whale, what would you say?"

"I ain't no snack."

"You think that's intelligent conversation?"

"Meaningful," said Tuktu.

The pelagic herdsmen rose, made their goodbyes, and left.

"Good luck," they said. "Maybe we'll see you out there."

"Thanks," said Kim.

The young hydronauts watched them out of sight.

"Why are you rubbing your ear, Kim?" asked Toby.

He stared at her. He was rubbing the ear unconsciously, then deliberately as though some alien sound had penetrated without his knowledge. He frowned. There was a sound, a chittering, trilling squeak of sorts, not definitely heard as normal hearing, but there. It was a signal of distress.

He spun on his heel and looked down the dock. A giant dolphin was broaching, leaping out of water as though clamoring for attention. He ran toward it as his companions looked at him with astonishment.

"Punch the hospital button on that emergency post," he commanded. "Get an ambulance squad down here. Tuktu, push the dockside alert for a fast first-aid work sub. No questions. Get going. There's trouble."

He sprinted toward the broaching dolphin. It looked like old Pudge, maybe it was Pudge, and all of them had worked with him in the kelp forests and the shark pens. But even if it weren't Pudge, it was telling him something important.

The squeaks and whistles ran down the sound range as Kim neared it, and at this distance, he didn't need any reception device to hear. He decoded automatically from long practice.

"Trouble," said the bottlenose. "Net collapsed

at end of Pen Area One. All divers outside work sub. One under attack and bleeding. Send help fast."

"Wait here and lead," said Kim, warbling with his mouth as he had done many times in the past without the usual undersea equipment that increased the range of messages. At this distance, almost head to head, he didn't need it.

There was a *whoosh* of water behind him as an emergency work sub ejected from its dockside ramp slid to a wave halt beside the dolphin.

Kim shouted at the heads popped from its open hatch.

"Trouble, bad trouble. Follow the dolph, and get cracking!"

Sub and cetacean vanished, and only two arrowing ripples marked their going. The nooning sun turned the subsiding wake into silver spear points, shining markers as direction clues into the seemingly peaceful bay.

There was much to be said for in-sea training and the deep, perceptive, twinlike intimacies of in-sea work teams sharing hard-tried friendships with their peers. Tuktu, Genright, and Toby Lee were relaxed and silent. They had functioned. They stayed loose and ready to act again. Whatever they thought remembering their own dangerous days beneath those pastel waters, they stayed mute. They didn't even turn when the hushed ambulance, moving on its solar-powered batteries, whispered to a stop beside them.

One of its attendants, noticing the extra little rank chevron on Kim's fatigues, moved toward him.

"You put the call in?"

"Right," snapped Kim.

"Funny we didn't get the emergency message from the bay."

"All outside the boat and very busy defending," answered Kim. "According to the dolphin. He brought the word."

"And just lucky you were here and knew the language, eh?"

"You'll get a report."

"Dolphin checked in, huh? And you with no face-mask receiver or anything, huh? You better make that report to the office. I think I'll take the ambulance home in case it's needed somewhere."

The attendant's voice was decidedly unpleasant. His shoulders humped in an ugly, defiant bunching.

"That doctor with you a good one?" asked Kim.

"What do you care?"

"Well, I hope so, because if you touch that

ambulance control, you'll need him real badly, and I want all his attention on the patients coming in."

It was more than a half-hour before the emergency work sub homed in to the dock and cracked its plexiglass hull. The men in it worked a stretcher litter out and up the ramp to the waiting ambulance, carefully and gently.

Kim watched the doctor make his preliminary inspection, then moved to see the occupant. Tuktu, Genright, and Toby Lee moved with him.

Together they saw the drawn, pale face of the boat loader they'd helped just a few hours earlier. He recognized them and tried to smile.

He waved toward the end of the litter. "Forgot to watch the one that wanted to play kissie-kissie," he whispered.

The blanket which covered him flattened abruptly at his right knee.

Genright stretched an impulsive hand to his shoulder.

"They'll give you a nifty new one like my arm," he said. "Ask for a black one."

The young warden was smiling faintly as the ambulance swished off, trailing a white wisp of coquina dust.

"Where are the rest of the net tenders?" Kim asked the rescue crew.

"Swimming in under their own steam," answered their leader. "Sub's tangled under the net and will have to be handled later. Swimmers have pulsars and hand laser units just in case, and they've got a hefty brace of dolphin escorts. Good thing you were around. Your alert was the only one we had, but then I imagine things got awfully busy very quickly down there at the time.

"Help us with the report, will you?" He grinned. "I guess the Base Commander already has it, knowing him."

"You can bet on it," said Toby Lee. "But we'll help."

"We'll be here until everybody's home," added Tuktu.

"They're not too far away," said one of the rescue team. "Shouldn't be long."

They weren't. The dolphins arrived first, and the big male *was* Pudge. Toby Lee recognized him by a dimple under his chin, a dimple with a shadowy goatee.

"How could you not know him?" she reproved Kim.

"Yeh, how could you not know him?" asked Genright. "How could you not know the female too? It's Peggy. She's got a dimple right under her chin with a tiny goatee."

The four of them hung over the dock and spoke eeeks and whistles with their old friends as the three other weary net tenders slopped out of the water and huddled with the rescue crew. They gave their heartfelt thanks to Kim and Tuktu and Genright and Toby Lee and made their way to the medical building adjacent to the docks.

"That's that," said Kim absently.

He felt Toby's hand slide into his. Tuktu's heavy arm suddenly weighed upon his shoulder, and Genright's black satin face moved against his nose.

"That is not that," they said in unison.

"We'd said goodbye to the open-range types, right? Right! You spun, started to run, and issued orders at the same time. Right? Right! You heard something we didn't, and our ears are as good, if not better than yours. Right? Right! You heard that dolphin, that's what. And you heard him just when I asked why you were rubbing your ear, I'll bet. So talk," demanded Toby.

"Maybe I wouldn't make so much of this," said Tuktu, "but those whale nurses had just finished talking about animal sound frequencies."

"High, low, detected and undetected ranges," added Genright.

"I think you heard something you couldn't hear," snapped Toby Lee.

"Well, I can hear Genright because his nose is rubbing mine," said Kim, shoving him away and pulling Toby closer so he could drape an arm across her. "But I think you all may be right, because I don't know exactly how I heard Pudge's signal, except I did."

"Then I think it might be useful if we sort of messed around the acoustical laboratories here this afternoon for a while," said Toby Lee. "You might have a special gift."

"I agree, and for some other reasons," said Kim. "What I would like, if it's possible, is some way to gimmick the communications between our boats, assuming that we're ordered to cruise and work together, so that we could have a com system of our very own. Commander Brent has already indicated that we'll be monitored, and that we'll have a set channel for our reports to the mother ship or another base. That make sense to us?"

"Does to me," said Tuktu. "We're all pretty good with the sensing business, but Genright's special with a lot of instruments. And he hung around with all those super-experts a lot while we were aboard that fancy *Polaris* when we were on Hawaii Search, you remember."

"Might be something I could pinch from the lab," Genright suggested sweetly.

"Not with my knowledge," Kim said firmly.

"Well, let's go," snorted Toby Lee. "I have a

feeling we aren't going to be on the base much longer."

Genright held up a warning hand. "Aren't we forgetting the one thing that would have the most influence on our futures?"

"I know," said Tuktu, "but only because I've lived with you so long. Lunch!"

Toby Lee giggled.

"Okay," said Kim. "Might as well go by the routines. And I think it might be sense to check by Commander Torrance's office for permission to use the sound labs as well. What's more, you know he'll want our version of this morning's emergency operations. You know him and Jiggs Jensen. They don't miss anything."

Kim was right. They had just finished their meal when the audio system summoned them to the headquarters office, where the two top Base executives awaited them.

Kim was brief with his report of the dockside events. The others were equally so with their affirmation of the same activities. But Kim was uneasy as they spoke. It was one thing to sense that he'd heard a normally unhearable sound from the dolphin and to share that suspicion with his brother-bonded friends and with Toby. He could never successfully hide anything from her anyhow. But Service training and Service conditioning was strong. Should he speculate with his commanding officers, even those as understanding as Commanders Torrance and Jensen? He felt that old warm intrusion of Toby's mind with his, felt her sympathetic concern. He also felt a deeper, more probing regard in the steady eyes of Commanders Torrance and Jensen. Not for the first time he realized that long years, and active years, in the Service builds strong intuitions.

"Fine," said Commander Torrance when Tuktu ended his report. "I'm putting you all in for a commendation on the venerable fitness records. You were there. You acted properly."

He paused. "Rockwell, you were quite a distance away from that dolphin when he surfaced, and according to all of you, your back was turned away from him, so you couldn't see him broach. Did you just happen to turn around by accident and catch a look?"

"What we mean," said Commander Jensen amiably, "is there anything else you want to tell us?"

Unconsciously Kim rubbed his ear. He made his decision. But there was a thin needle of sensation in his head that broke into tiny splinters of sound, and the sound stretched, snapped, stretched and snapped almost as though it were patterned into code.

"He heard that dolphin," said Toby Lee firmly.

"He's hearing something else right now," said Commander Jensen.

"You," muttered Tuktu.

"No, he's right," said Kim. "But not hearing exactly, like, very like, but, but . . ."

"Out of normal human sound range, however, well above," said Commander Jensen. He stuck a huge hand into a capacious pocket and pulled out a boxlike cube. "Transmitter set about one twenty kilocycles. We got to thinking about that incident on the dock. Then we got to thinking about your conversation with the herdsmen we sent down to chat with you about sound.

"We did ask them to check back with us, you know.

"Then, I guess, we just got to thinking in general. We do a lot more of that around here, in case you ever get to wondering why we sit so much. And when we added up that dock story, it added up to some super-hearing acuity for Rockwell.

"We're not stupid as in plain stupid. This thing could be a freak, a one-time happening, or anything. That's why we ran the little transmitter test.

"And, you, Rockwell heard it. Not me. Nobody else. Just you. Right?" Commander Jensen was downright accusing.

"I'm not really sure, sir," said Kim. "It's more like the suspicion of hearing than . . . well, I'm not convinced I'm hearing. And while we're on the subject, we were going to ask if we might use the acoustical labs this afternoon, just sort of to noodle with things?"

"Permission granted," said Commander Torrance. He swiveled in his chair and looked through his window to the sea. He grunted. "If you want something, requisition it even if it's small enough to fit in a pocket." He grunted again, turned, and faced them. His thin face looked suddenly older, somehow more tired.

"Orders," he said. "You are leaving here tomorrow early for Olympia Base again to pick up your boats and equipment. Commander Brent will meet you there for final briefings and final sea checks on boat and equipment handling.

"One word. Don't let the inventory clerks check off your gear. Do it yourself with them, especially your personal diving suits and weaponry.

"And another word, and strictly in this office. We don't have to tell you how important this over-all mission is. If there are sea-adapted people in major numbers using the oceans, they'll be allies or enemies, depending upon our treatment of them. It's all right for us to say that they are human in everything but form and that they have a right to survival. They were created to be men of the world's waters because some of our best ancestors thought there could no longer be men of land."

Commander Torrance made a small honking noise.

"So, as far as the record goes, men created these men because they *were* men and wanted to assure the life of their own kind. Well, Jiggs and I want to tell you that the micro-archives and history tapes of the cities aren't exactly complete. An awful lot of good stuff was cut out of the history books to justify an awful lot of the bad necessary to save humanity. But some of it was saved, and is still believed."

He patted a small glassine-bound old-fashioned book, a book with real pages designed to be read.

"There are more of these around than you might think," he said. "I have one for each of your teams. The Book was once called the Bible. I guess you could call it a fairy tale history of a very ancient people who thought that man needed something more to think about than his own manhood.

"Read it or not as you please. Jiggs and I are

pretty fond of you kids, and it gets mighty big and lonesome out where you're going. Good luck."

They saluted formally and spun for the door.

Commander Jensen's voice was lazy at their backs.

"If we find out whether or not we had a visitor the other night, we'll ask him why he came to call," it said.

4

Winter was nibbling at the temperate zones. Far to the north, along the escarpments of what had once been the Aleutian island chain, and westward, into the Bering Sea, the icy floods of the Arctic Ocean were choking in new ice, locked bergs, and fresh snows.

The gray whales had begun their annual migration to the warm waters of the southlands. They were stuffed and fat with north Pacific plankton, the pteropods that looked like sea butterflies, the calanus called the "water flea," and all the krill or whale food they had grazed under the summer sun.

They were headed south to frolic, to mate and give birth to babies whose natal blubber was so thin they would surely have died from the chilled seas of the northern ranges. They were headed south in pairs, pods, and herds because a biologic clock set forty million years ago said it was time to move to bluer, greener, and sunnier ocean areas and calving lagoons. It was time to butt and sport, to sound and breach, to blow water from their twin blowholes—water that looked like water instead of iced mist as they breathed.

And it was time to scoop trenches in the near shore shallows with huge jaws that engulfed bottom worms, clams, shrimps, small fish, and even plain mud. Everything would be strained through their hairy baleen filters before the yummies were swallowed and the rest ejected by a surge of whale tongues.

The grays were not among the prettier beasts. These, larger than their pre-nuclear-war ancestors, measured some sixty to eighty feet along barely tapered, comparatively slender cylindrical bodies which were powered by horizontal flukes some fifteen feet across their trailing edges. Their heads were long and nosy. Almost a third of their bodies were marine ghettos inhabited by colonies of barnacles and crablike whale lice which contributed to the mottled gray color of the skin. That skin was crisscrossed with old scars. It looked as though it had been tacked to the whale's underlying blubber in patches.

The hydronauts had been among them nearly a month, Kim and Toby Lee in their work sub *Adam I*, and Tuktu and Genright in *Adam II*. Their sailing from Olympia Base had been almost casual after another series of craft operational tests and supply and equipment loadings.

Commander Brent had appeared, been curt with a few last-minute good luck grumbles, handed over an envelope of orders to each crew, and had vanished again. A variety of senior Service types had arrived, apparently just to say hello and mumble about kids being given the newest and best of the fleet work subs. And Genright had collected a clutch of what appeared to be school children who did mysterious things to the communications systems of both boats while laughing wildly and jabbing themselves in the ribs as they played. But when the children had finished, *Adam I* and *II* obviously had their own talk-between-ships arrangements, and exclusive ones.

"Very tight beam stuff," said Genright. "Range up to infinity."

"You know what you're talking about?" asked Tuktu.

"All done with the buttons," explained Genright loftily.

Kim and Toby Lee had found some time to spend in the huge Base library files, with Kim particularly interested in the low sound frequencies which traveled farther than the high frequencies, and Toby Lee fascinated by some musty knowledge of human languages that were once whistled instead of spoken.

"Look," she told Kim. "A language called Mazateco once used in a place called Mexico, a language called Silbo-Gomero used in the Canary Islands, and a third called Aas used in the Pyrenees mountains of some place named Spain. No words. All whistles . . . much like dolphins. Give you any ideas?"

Tuktu, his broad brown face impassive, had a present printed on a large roll of shark parchment for Genright. It said anything done for the cause of compatability is not only condoned but required. It had a cartoon picture of Genright with big knives sticking out of his chest, knees, and shoulders, and a fat lump on his head.

"It's a nice likeness," said Genright.

Kim chuckled at the thought, and he watched the sea, calm and mirrorlike before the bow of *Adam I*. The sub was riding high, its gray-green weldglass hull bobbing like a lazy cork. The boat, he thought, never seemed to bother the whales. Why should it? Its thirty feet was just little more than the size of a nursing calf as far as the herds were concerned. And once the roving pods had satisfied their members that the work craft was not a predator like the killer whale, the orca, and was too large to be strained through baleen, it was ignored—mostly.

Not a predator? Not exactly, thought Kim, amused.

Adam I and *Adam II* were merely very dangerous under special circumstances. They carried pulsars which could be sonic weapons, hand lasers, and fixed installations of the same heat-light beams. There were small arsenals of nerve gases in drop sizes which could kill or stun for miles over open ocean. There were small round algin containers of chemicals, tiny enough to fit into one of Toby Lee's palms, that could thump out a blast which would make a frappe out of a sizable iceberg.

The seed-size A-power plant which supplied

the boat's inner comforts and general sea efficiency was designed for life use of the compact vessel. And the sensing equipment and communications systems, properly used, brooded twenty-four hours daily, using light, heat, chemical, visual, aural analytical techniques to supply a steady flow of information of all environmental surroundings. That equipment was the tools of the trade.

"Toby," he said. "Dead ahead."

He saw her nod slightly.

A female gray breached from the still sea and rolled over in mid-air so her back would take the impact of the inevitable wallop landing. She was followed by two males in mating pursuit, and she was obviously ready to be caught. One of them surged over her head and forced her to the surface in a giant swirl of agitated sea. As they joined, belly to belly, sides tilted upward to the sky, the third male gray skidded over the foreparts of their bodies and stabilized them. His weight held them firmly in position during their brief act of leviathan love, then his comradely assistance no longer needed, he dived away, leaving husband and wife to their own monagamous future. It would be a year and another trip north before the pair would return and the cow would give birth.

"Some process," said Kim inanely, to hide the

fact that he had been truly impressed by a wondrous act of nature among giants.

"Well," said Toby Lee tartly, "from some points of view the show would have been improved by fewer characters. One less, at least."

"The female," said Kim, and swayed out of the reach of her swatting arm.

"Hardly," she snapped.

Tuktu's voice on the *Adam*-only intercom filled the con area.

"We're clearing for permission to leave the boat," it said. "You can see us half a mile south lined to our own ring buoy right now. Seems to be a lot of dolphins playing around the herd. They may be working, of course. But we thought we'd take a look. We're using heavy shield suits just in case we get bumped a bit, but the water's right quiet and all the big animals are docile. What do you think?"

Kim was snappish.

"Stay in the boat. That's an order. You get mixed up in a mating ritual, and you might find trouble."

"That's what I told Genright when he left twenty minutes ago," Tuktu said calmly.

"You stay put," said Kim. "We'll be along. We're under orders not to interfere with regular herd operations, and those dolphins may be cutting out an animal for a reason that doesn't concern us."

"That's what I told Genright before he said his com unit wasn't working very well."

"How's it working now, Genright?" asked Kim suddenly.

"Fine. Ooops!"

"Back to the boat," ordered Kim.

"Soon as I finish with old Tube Steak," said Genright. "Only be a minute."

"Old what?" asked Toby Lee.

"He has a pet, an old bull. Calls it Tube Steak," explained Tuktu. "And I forgot to tell you, I'm in the water too, and the dolphins are cutting out a yearling bull from the procession."

"Wait a minute. How does he know Tube Steak is a pet?" asked Toby Lee, throwing up her hands.

"He has kind eyes," interrupted Genright's voice. "I'm looking into one of them."

"Am returning to boat," said Tuktu, "but will watch over the dark one."

"You're both going on report for discipline anyhow," Kim snapped irritably.

"Might as well finish up here then," rattled Genright's voice.

"Up here" was not a figure of speech. It was a fact of literal action. When Toby Lee arrived in

Adam 1, Genright, mask and helmet tilted on the back of his head, was on his hands and knees just behind the twin blowholes of the biggest, hoariest old man of a bull gray whale they had ever seen. Genright had a huge clam shell in a two-handed grip of his gloved hands. He was scraping patches of cog-shaped barnacles off the monster's back, pausing now and then to brush them into the sea.

The whale, some seventy feet of him, was motionless in the placid ocean, some fixed dream in his open eyes, and a silly delphine grin, more pronounced than the usual, on his long snout. As Genright worked, the skin along his back rippled, bunched, and folded.

"Tickly, tickly, kitchy, kitchy," shouted Genright.

"That's ridiculous," said Kim. "Insane!"

Toby Lee's laughter tinkled up the sonic scales to near-hysteria. She nearly rolled off the stool before the bank of visual scanners.

The big bull moved ever so slightly forward and submerged about five feet, ducking Genright but apparently taking pains not to dislodge him.

"He's just washing off the dust and stuff," explained Genright. "I got to work out some kind of scraper or a rake or something to do his belly right. He's pretty crummy."

The whale rose slowly, water rolling off his back. Where Genright had scraped his skin was sleek and pearly.

Genright stood up, adjusted his mask and helmet, immediately improving communications with the two nearby craft. "Whee!" he yelled, sat and slid, rump first, down the whale's side into the sea. He swam around to the nearest eye and patted the area behind it.

"Be back later, Tube Steak."

"You forgot to get paid," said Tuktu's rich voice.

"Well, when I first met him I thought he was going to eat me. I pumped a real low note of pulsar at him, and he changed his mind—just from surprise, I guess. So he's got credit with me. Besides there's no pay for anything in the Service. All the job materials are free too. Thirty feet under old Tube Steak the bottom's full of big shells."

The gray made a slow turn and followed Genright's swimming form back to *Adam II*. It nosed at the boat, gently and tentatively. Then it sculled over to *Adam I* and did the same thing. Without haste it moved off toward the south, angling out to the horizon line.

"Tuktu, you still suited?" asked Kim. "If you

are, join us in *Adam One.* You hear that, Genright?"

"Right. Coming."

"We'll crack the stern pressure bubble, and we can talk without your coming all the way in and slopping up our housekeeping. Handle the bubble, please, Toby. I've got a small idea."

He moved toward the bow communications board as he spoke, and poked a finger at the area range band. "*This is Adam One,* Rockwell."

"You're on, Rockwell," said a soft voice. "This is Herd Base Area C. Knew you were around. What can we do for you?"

"Keep me from being too ignorant mostly," said Kim. "What I want to know is, well, do any of the grays get disturbed, maybe even nasty, at divers operating near or around them?"

"Swimmers are forbidden anywhere in the sea near or around the herds unless under specific emergency conditions and direct operating instructions. Benthic samplers work the in-coast areas occasionally, or biologists may be tagging special animals for migration records. Once in a blue moon there may be a predator emergency which might necessitate swimmers in the waters. But your answer is that the grays could be difficult and react as unpredictably as any animal that finds something new and strange in his environment. You may see our power kayaks around, but we don't encourage swimmers. And you know it.

"None of you have been swimming, have you?" The voice was syrupy, yet firm.

"Yes," said Kim steadily, "and I'll so report."

"The dolphins ratted on you, you know."

"Real gossips, aren't they? But I think we'll be back in the water again from time to time—with caution, of course. Thought you ought to know."

"Your orders don't come from us," said the voice, "but thanks for checking in, and anything you see that's interesting or possibly helpful to us, cut us in."

"Thank you," said Kim.

He went aft. The uplifted faces of Genright and Tuktu smiled from the water held level in the hatch well by the in-boat pressure like two beaming vegetables in a clear soup. Toby Lee squatted beside them, a barefooted idol in shorts and a nondescript halter.

"Discipline first," said Kim. "As long as I wear one more stripe, you check in first when you have your whims. You'll both be on report, and it'll look nasty on your records. Too bad. Shouldn't have been swimming."

He paused, but before they could speak, he went on.

"When the three of you go out again tomorrow, wear silco skin suits and use the mantles just in case you need a lot of sudden speed."

Kim was talking about the silco-membrane diving suits which literally fitted like a skin with an inner lining of pore-penetrating hair follicles which converted the oxygen in the water directly into the blood stream and simultaneously removed the carbon dioxide so the wearer could breathe as a true fish. The mantle, patterned after the natural ones of the squids, was a flexible armored tube which contracted and expanded by power units that "inhaled" and "ejected" water for bursts of jet propulsion.

Tuktu looked stunned.

"You put us on report for swimming in the herds, foul up our Service records, then you send us out again?"

"Wait a minute, chunky buddy," said Genright thoughtfully.

Toby Lee merely smiled quietly.

"Herd Base Area C said the whales don't like strange objects messing around," continued Kim. "The dolphins they take because they are used to being banged around by them, I guess. Anyhow, what's a one-ton slam when it bangs sixty-seventy-eighty tons? But you know what you were doing to that Tube Steak, and he didn't seem to mind a bit. I sort of got the idea that he might be used to handling or used to being handled by something or body your size or your general shape."

"That's farfetched thinking," said Toby Lee.

Kim exploded. "How farfetched do you think this whole mission is? Just what do you think our percentage of stumbling over any of the sea people is if they wanted to hide in all the world's oceans? And I don't care how many Service people are searching. Come on now. Just what do you think the real odds against us are?"

"Oh, I think our chances of finding them are fine," said Genright. "Farfetched thinking, you know."

"We'll wind up back in the cities being brain-scrubbed and working on a mushroom farm," muttered Tuktu.

"Very good too," said Genright.

"May I ask what's very good?" asked Toby.

"Tube Steak and mushrooms," guffawed Genright.

"With black marks on our records too," continued Tuktu.

"If you had any brains, you'd know I had to put you on report. The working dolphins turned you in to Herd Command."

"You just think of that?" asked Toby suspiciously.

"I'll ignore that," said Kim.

"Thought you would."

"All right, Genright, let's have the whole Tube Steak story, and without frills, just as it happened—what you did and what the bull did."

Genright was succinct. He and Tuktu had noticed the dolphin activity, and Genright had decided to enter the sea and investigate although they knew it was doubtless a herd routine. The big bull gray had surfaced before him, swimming like an island conjured from thin air. It had opened its mouth. But, and Genright was sure, it wasn't about to scoop him within it. He had touched off the pulsar tube, and it had emitted a low note just once.

"Sort of a nice moo real deep," he elaborated.

The whale had closed its mouth and remained still and awash.

Genright had swum under it, around it, and noticing the barnacles, some of which had drawn blood from the whale's skin, he had pulled a few loose. He had dived to the bottom—the water was comparatively shallow there—and returned with the big clam shell. It was easy climbing up on the whale even with his fins because the encrustations offered a foothold and a handgrip. He wasn't sure, but he thought maybe the whale had lowered itself in the water a bit to make it easier for him. That's when he told Tuktu he had a pet. And that's all there was to it until Kim got nasty.

"Touch that low-frequency note on the pulsar for us," said Kim.

Genright drew the tube from its contained slot in the thigh of his suit. It did make a sound, low and mooing within the confines of the boat. Sound is only a signal, and it would have not been that quiet in the water, which is a better conductor than air.

The pulsar tubes and their larger variations were used extensively for moving and guiding fish, all of which are sensitive to sound. They were used a lot in the shark pens, where they had a commanding effect on that strange band of nerves encircling the shark bodies and known as the lateral line.

But whales had no lateral lines. If anything, their entire bodies were huge baffles, sounding boards absorbing all sorts of noises.

Kim shrugged.

"I still think that gray acted pally as though he were at ease with a buddy," he said. "As if he were used to being handled."

"So we go out tomorrow at the same time and same place, which is right here, and see if he turns up again for another treatment? That's a really magic idea," said Tuktu bluntly.

"Toby goes too," added Kim. "She's still a different form in size and shape than each of you."

"When did you first notice?"

"Not that whale vision is anything much. Those grays have to breach for a quick scan around them, although their eyes work better underwater. But if he gets you in sonic range with his echo system clicking away, he'll notice the differences."

"Suppose, Mr. Rockwell, sir, we decide that Tube Steak is used to being handled. What does that prove?"

"That something has handled him," snapped Kim.

"Not another whale, nor a dolphin, nor a shark, nor a skate, nor an albalone, nor an urchin, nor a sea otter . . ." muttered Genright.

"Nor a cod, nor a tuna, nor an eel, nor a pilchard, nor Commander Brent, nor Toby Lee . . ." murmured Tuktu.

Their faces vanished from the wall.

Toby buttoned up the bubble and the hatch.

5

The sun blazing through the broad west window which formed most of one wall of Commander Torrance's headquarters office at Baja Base added little heat compared with that already in the room. Not surprisingly, most of that heat was generated by the ice in the glacial tones of Commander Brent's measured speech.

"I don't have enough trouble with this forlorn-hope operation. Oh no, not near enough. The Council members who have to know about it are divided between those seeing nothing and those seeing ghosts of old wars or worse.

"By order of the Council Controller the members who don't know about the search are to be kept from knowing it for the duration—and thank goodness we loaded it with survey work of all types which had to be done sooner or later anyhow—so security is fairly tricky all around.

"Then there's the little matter of establishing a trusted network from the Kuril Islands to Unameit and equipping and staffing. But that's not enough trouble. No trouble at all. That's my job.

"But then what? Or what then? Why, practically nothing. Just sailing along through regular channels and open to every little security null at a desk comes a report of two senior Service officers and four rebel wardens about to find and ask some strange sea creatures for help in taking over the social system. And how could this be? Have the genetic controls failed? Have all the psychological sciences gone daft? Have all the rules by which we live become empty? Is discipline and pride in the Service gone?

"You can just see it. Up through the regular channels of Service administration and management comes this report. It is copied. It is marked and recorded. All the clerks in the offices waggle their tongues, but fortunately only to each other. Then, in due time, the report reaches me, and back down all the channels it goes with the word that the matter is fully processed and action taken.

"But that's what I need more of, trouble. Nothing small. Just treason, rebellion, high crime against the society's survival.

"Who is Warden Second Class Petrie Putnam, Hive Number 11100, Lab Lot XYY2, Nursery Number 42859, Service Number 44456, Grade Training 6, assigned to Baja Base Shark Pens?"

The purple flush on Commander Tod Torrance's cheeks had faded.

"He is a nice, efficient young man, perfectly conditioned for his social function, nicely trained for his work, beautifully disciplined enough even to please you. He should be commended for the courage it took to submit such a report," said Torrance.

"He is a lad with big ears," growled Jiggs Jensen, "who accidentally overheard talk which startled him coming from fellow wardens and senior officers. He slams doors."

"That doesn't excuse either of you," snapped Commander Brent. "I've known you two for thirty years or more, so tell me about such talk in detail."

"We'll let you hear it," said Commander Tod Torrance. "And just among us, which includes you, Brent, it might remind you of talk I heard from us that thirty or more years ago you were recalling."

"Don't look surprised," said Jiggs Jensen. "We keep records after our fashion, particularly on people that are going to replace our sort as custodians of the Service."

He thumbed a desk button, and Commander Brent, listened, nodded, and finally shook his head as though he'd heard voices whistling down the corridors of time from some very personal past.

"Shocking," he said, pursing his lips.

"What?" asked Commander Torrance.

Commander Brent rubbed a hand over his face and, with the gesture, seemingly discarded a mask long cultivated with care and patience. He grinned like a small child.

"That they should be so smart so young," he said. "I think the world's going to make it. I also notice that you old hard-shells gave them reading matter."

"Which reminds me, speaking of reading matter where is young Warden Putnam's report at present?" asked Tod Torrance directly.

"Where it won't give us trouble at the present," answered Commander Brent. He stiffened into his usual high-authority presence. "I shall commend young Putnam for his high sense of duty, as you suggested. But the fact remains that the matter is on the official record. It could mean serious trouble for Rockwell, Lee, Selsor, and Barnes any time if it were revived for almost any cause, although your so-called records of the session would be helpful to all of you. It could be trouble for both of you as well. But from what I've seen of them and my own judgment of them, those youngsters are always on the thin edge of disciplinary problems. Comes from thinking and imagination.

"From their check-in reports they ought to be somewhere off your coasts right about now. Should they think well enough of you to call despite orders to contact only specified stations, you may tell them anything you see fit to tell them about, except me. And need I remind you that other ears are always listening."

He rose.

Approximately eighty-odd miles west under a flawless sky on a breezeless day, with a sea so calm it looked painted in place, rose Tube Steak. He was not and then he was, so quietly did he ease his bulk to the surface. He had fed, and perhaps not too long ago, from some hospitable area of the ocean floor. Festoons of weed hung from his jaws like rejected salad. There was a blotch of some claylike sediment under his chin. He was not alone, for, as he snorted a languid sigh aloft in a barely visible jet of vapor, another bull eased from the water beside him. He too breathed a limp, completely unworthy fountain, and silently lined himself at Tube Steak's side.

"Well, well, well," said Genright, "old T. Steak with Tube Two, and right on time as expected by our leader, if not me."

"Never mind the theories. You might have known he'd be back to have his afternoon massage," said Toby Lee.

"If he thinks I'm going to start a cleaning station for him and his kooky buddies, he needs two more holes in the top of his skull," said Genright, burbling grimly into his facepiece.

"*Adam One*, you got us under close scan?" interrupted Tuktu. "All I see from here is a cliff of whale."

"Scanned, and prepared for possible naughtiness." Kim's voice from *Adam I* was cheerful.

"He's pleased with himself," muttered Toby. "*Adam One*, what do we do now?"

"Swim around them. Let 'em get familiar with you."

"Nobody gets familiar with me," snapped Toby Lee.

"Tube Steak's friend has a spaghetti batch of remora on his belly. I think he'd like 'em off," said Kim.

Many cetaceans and other larger forms of life in the oceans are beset by parasites like the remora, a small fish with a suckerlike mouth that attaches itself to some host and lives on its bounty of flesh and blood. Temperature changes remove most of them from migrating animals like the grays, and they wiggle off weakly in warmer waters to be eaten by cruising predators. But they are tenacious, and hold fast in most instances until the whale itself scrapes them off against the bottom or rocks.

The three hydronauts in the sea vanished from the placid surface. The bull grays sent a barely noticeable quiver along their stabilizing pectoral fins, which were about fourteen feet long and roughly four or five wide, and floated blissfully.

"You're right, Kim," said Genright's voice on the com hookup, "Tube Two needs a tummy shave."

"I'm going up on T. Steak's back," said Toby Lee. "He likes me. He's winked at me twice."

"He's measuring you," said Tuktu. "Wants to know if you'll strain down nice between all those hairies hanging from his baleen plates before he puts those jaws around you."

"Anyhow, I'm getting a shell and going up."

"Tuktu," ordered Kim. "Sort of mess around with that pair. Touch 'em even where you think it might be sensitive. Try and get a feel of whether or not they've been . . . well, sort of accustomed to something like you. Know what I mean?"

"I choose not to know what you mean," said Tuktu pompously. "What kind of an order is that? Mess and poke and see what happens. I notice you're safe and comfortable in the boat."

"I'm scanning and recording both audio and visual for your accident reports," laughed Kim.

There was a *whoosh*ing churn of ripples, and Tube Two disappeared.

"Yep," said Genright. "He's sensitive right there. Come back Tube. Here Tutu, Tutu, Tutu . . . I'm not going to chase you."

"What d'y'know? He's coming back too," said Tuktu.

"Wow!" cried Genright underwater. "That click of his is enough to deafen a person."

"He's coming, all right," barked Tuktu, "and he's going too. Mighty fast."

Tube Steak vanished, dunking Toby, and boiled off behind Tube Two.

"They've picked up trouble," Kim's voice said steadily. "Shark. Looks like a white. Face south and expect him at eleven o'clock. Fan out a bit. Genright and Tuktu, be ready with hand lasers. Toby, use the pulsar set high. Sound alone may be enough to stop him. But be alert. If I tell you to jet out of there on your mantles, you scatter. I can always use the boat weapons, and they're ready now."

"When do we get a look at him?" asked Toby Lee calmly.

"Any minute now," said Kim. "He's three hundred feet away from you, now two, one, and ought to be in sight in this water—right now!"

The white shark, one of the great predators, moved like a shadow, easily, gracefully, and swiftly. The early years of radiation-steeped seas had caused drastic size mutations among most of the selachians.

This one, not excessively large among his peers, might have measured some forty feet, but like all of his clan he came hungry and dangerous to anything that might make an item on his all-embracing menu. He would have taken fifty-pound bites out of the whales, which could defend themselves only by lashing about with their flukes or by breaching in the vain hope that their crashing weight might land upon an unwary foe.

The great white paused as it neared the swimmers as though choosing a target.

Toby Lee thumbed the pulsar tube.

Scent may be the keenest of senses within the many species of sharks, but it is followed closely by sound, which sharks almost literally "hear" with their nerve ends.

Toby, a veteran of work in the shark pens, as were all the other hydronauts, had set the pulsar beam to a most unpleasant frequency, which, magnified by the water medium through which it passed, turned the white into a circle.

For a moment its pea brain restrained the killer instinct generated by forever hunger and weighed it against acute discomfort. The latter would have meant nothing to any shark in a feeding frenzy. But this one apparently sought an easier meal. It flicked an immense caudal fin, veered off, and slipped away swiftly westward to deeper waters. Had it not, the lasers held by Tuktu and Genright would have sliced it into a mess of food for smaller fishes.

Killing is not a casual matter in the Service. It is waste if it does not produce raw materials for the survival of the cities. Or survival of the Service staff members.

"Well done," rapped Kim's voice.

"Hark at the cozy leader," said Genright. "Did you log that incident?"

"Everything is logged. Comment?"

"Just wanted to make sure you had how bravely and resolutely I faced the enemy."

"Jet mantle set to full power for instant flight," said Tuktu.

"It is true that I am a man who thinks," muttered Genright.

"Let's think about the big tubes," said Toby Lee. "Any sign of them, Kim?"

"Not only sign, but sight and sound presence," said *Adam 1*. "They are coming back, and I don't care who disagrees, that's proof enough for me that Tube Steak and Tube Two are not strangers to . . . all I can think of is handling, but I could mean guidance or even protection. And by swimmers, not Service people, just swimmers, your size maybe.

"If you want to know, I'm thinking about the biological attacks on our people during Hawaii Search, and that crazy whale that tried to ram the *Polaris* on the same mission. Something or somebody or some built-in signal turned just plain fish into weapons then to protect the hatch of sea babies. And I'm saying that Steak and Two are suspect, at least in my mind."

"Talk later," said Tuktu's voice. "Arrivals have arrived."

"Well, hello, Tube Steak, did you have a nice run?" asked Genright, cooing. "And you, old Tutu, back for belly cleaning?"

The pair of bull grays surfaced and indicated a slight surface zephyr by exhaling noisily. The baby breeze blew their own spray over their glistening backs. They bobbed as though there were never a shark in the oceans.

The hydronauts worked on them for more than a half-hour. Tube Steak was scraped of more barnacles. Tube Two was shorn of many parasites.

A wind freshened and splintered the mirror sea. Small swells began to hump from the southwest.

"Let's bring us all home," said Kim. "Weather's making. I don't want our *Adams* on anchor buoys. Return now and we'll move west to deeper water and then talk some more about Genright's pals."

Kim thought a moment. He thumbed at the console before him. "Calling Herd Base Area C," he said softly.

"Have you, *Adam One*," replied the syrupy voice, "been swimming again?"

"One great white shark has," said Kim evenly. "He tried for a snack off two old bull grays here and was discouraged. He moved away due west of this position. I suppose your people know he's around, but then I thought I'd report it anyhow."

"Thank you, Rockwell," said the remote voice. "That particular shark is now part of the day's haul. Assume the grays are fine?"

"Well and docile. They seem to be old-timers and remarkably friendly. Would you know them?"

"Offhand I'd say we do. That's without seeing them, of course. But if they've survived to be old-timers, they sound like retired pod leaders that we've allowed to survive for one good reason or other. But your term 'docile' doesn't sound quite right. Those bulls get to be eighty years old or so, they get a mite feisty too. Personally, I doubt if any of our people have been near them for years.

"Tell you what you can do if they seem to be part of your project—whatever that is. Pump a sleep pill into them and see if they carry a tattoo number along the trailing edge of their pectorals, that is, if it's visible by now. Give me the numbers and I'll give you a history."

"Thank you, sir," said Kim. "But it's no big thing right now."

"Call any time, *Adam One*."

"I'm home," said Toby Lee.

"Missed you," said Kim.

"Slipped our line and brought in the buoy, too."

"Tuktu and Genright home too?"

"Probably all buttoned up and ready by now."

"Out of your clothes, little one . . ."

"Sir?"

"And into your work garb. We're moving right now."

The two work subs headed out of the shallows westward scant miles to where the shelf ended with a drop into two thousand feet of ocean, scattering a wide variety of life with their easy movement: tuna, anchovies, schools of small squid, solitary sharks, and smaller fishes. The water was warm, light struck to some hundred and fifty feet, and murky in patches with a variety of plankters, many of them sown as old earth farmers once scattered seed, by the pelagic whale herders as food for their baleen charges.

The work sub sensing equipment recorded oceanic data as the boats moved to be analyzed and reported by the hydronauts as part of the daily work schedules.

They huddled *Adams I* and *II* over deep ocean some fifty feet from the surface, adjusting keel trim and boat buoyancy below the wave turbulence beginning to make with the rising winds on the surface.

And they talked on their own private com systems.

"I'm convinced those bulls are familiar with friends that are not members of the Service," said Kim. "Herd Base admits that its people might know them, even claims that they might be tagged and numbered. But the fella I talked with doubts if any of his herdsmen have been near them for years or, at least, since they were judged to be not meat. He gave me the impression that they were retired, sort of kept around to maintain migration confidence like old uncles. But what do you think? Tuktu?"

"They're used to being handled, I'd say. Otherwise they'd be nasty. As a pretty general rule, old animals just don't like being annoyed—"

"But handled by what?" interrupted Genright. "You remember Commander Brent said that the experts thought the second hatch, the whatevers we're looking for, were assumed to be delphine, more like big dolphins or porpoise variations. We don't look like that in the water. Not with four appendages—two arms, two legs—not counting gear."

"Well, suppose the new sea people don't look

like what the experts think they might look like?" asked Toby Lee. "Nobody's seen them. Only the last hatch, our sea babies."

"I could be plain wrong, too," said Kim. "Those old whales just might be cozy to get the gunk off their hides. Just enjoying some instinct for a symbiotic relationship like cleansing fish cleaning up other fish on a reef."

"Should we follow them around the herds and see what catches up to them?" asked Toby.

"I say ignore them," said Genright. "If they want to be buddies, let them look us up."

"Agree," snapped Tuktu. "We've plenty work to do, according to our manual of instructions, besides swabbing down gray whales."

"How would you feel about checking in with Baja Base and asking for some advice?" asked Kim.

"That's open communications," said Toby Lee. "And after all, theories are theories, and no sense in sounding sillier than we are."

"How do we know that Commanders Torrance and Jensen want to hear from us anyhow?" asked Genright.

"I know," said Kim firmly, and he could feel Toby's warm agreement in that curious interplay of minds they shared.

"So do I," said Tuktu slowly. "And what's

more, I think it might be a good idea if we gave them our private com call."

"I knew you were going to say that," said Genright.

"How?"

"I received a sudden message. It said Tuktu is a big blabber that can't keep a secret."

"Okay, we call Baja Base. But how do we give the skippers our com frequency?" demanded Kim. "Without giving it to any other listening monitor, if any?"

Toby Lee laughed. "I know," she said. And rose from her seat at the console, padded across the cabin, and took a book from a shelf atop her bunk.

"That's the Bible," said Kim.

"We heard that," came the voices of Tuktu and Genright simultaneously.

"Calling Baja Base, Baja Base," said Kim clearly. "This is Rockwell in *Adam One*, repeat *Adam One*, for Commander Torrance."

There was a hum and a short breath of waiting in both work subs, and then Commander Torrance's voice eased into the boats.

"Hello, Rockwell, and I assume associates. Commander Jensen is with me. We had a feeling you might be checking in. How is it with the whales?"

"We'll tell you, sirs, but first Toby Lee has a message for you."

Toby's voice was serene.

"Job forty-one, sirs," she said, "and the number of the verse which reads, 'He maketh the deep to boil like a pot; he maketh the sea like a pot of ointment.' Add two zeros for our private frequency."

"Stand by, wardens," said Commander Jensen's soft tones, a chuckle hidden in them.

The open com network went dead, and then the private speakers that Genright and his friends had played with at Olympia Base, and which the hydronauts had been using before Kim went to open net, became activated again.

"Very good," said Commander Jensen, "thirty-one hundred kilocycles, eh? Not likely anyone would be playing around except some lonely kayak driver on that band. Well, out with the report, young wardens."

6

There was wind on the surface, and banks of heavy wet clouds formed along the western horizon to bulwark off the sky. The swells mounted and adorned their tops with swirls of tiny bubbles as they humped toward the far eastern shoreline.

The automatic sensing systems in the work

subs noted the fading light at their depth although visibility within the craft never seemed to alter unless changed manually.

Kim spoke at length. He told Commanders Torrance and Jensen about Genright's experience with Tube Steak and the arrival of Tube Two. He described their work with, and upon, the old gray bulls. He recounted his theories about recognition by the whales of possibly alien strangers. He told of his checks with Herd Base.

From time to time the others interrupted with their own comments and guesses.

"Interesting," said Commander Torrance finally, "but you'd be awfully lucky so early in the game to have something really firm—"

"They are lucky," interrupted Commander Jensen. "They maketh the sea to boil like a pot. But tell me, is it likely that your pets will seek you out again? If so, I'd suggest you mark them somehow. Not a mural, Genright, but vividly so you might be able to follow them visually when the herds go north again, for instance."

"I'm sure they'll be around again, sir," said Genright.

"We'll find a way to mark them," said Kim.

"Now I have some other news." Commander Torrance's voice was almost his command tone. "We had a visitor the night you all heard the door slam here," he said. "Would any of you know a Warden Second Class Petrie Putnam?"

"No, sir," said the hydronauts.

Commander Torrance told them as much as he deemed necessary of the consequences of their overheard conversation.

"I want your work to be commendable in all phases," he added, "and your conduct the same under all circumstances. You know how the Service handles disaffection, and er, umph, any remote implications of tampering with controls and command chains. I won't even think the word 'treason.' But enough for now. Rockwell, don't drop your theories, try to think them through and document them.

"Check with us again when you can. And it may be that we shall be in touch with you."

"Job forty-one," said Commander Jensen. "'He maketh a path to shine after him. . . .' That's the next verse. Follow it. Out."

There was a flickering halt of time as though the hydronauts had simultaneously decided to hold breath for a moment.

"You heard the man," said Kim, dropping his words carefully. "Any suggestions?"

"Just follow the whales," muttered Tuktu.

"How do we mark Tube Steak so to bring out the blue in his eyes?" added Genright.

"Make him false eyelashes—red," Toby Lee said sweetly.

"Dye, just violent yellow dye," said Kim softly, "right into his old blubber hide and surface. The same stuff we use to mark off sea survey areas or buoy sites for relocation of buoys after storms. We've canisters of the stuff, laboratory anilines, and it lasts and lasts. We can try injections—the old tubes won't feel it—or smear it on around the caudal areas so the south view of northbound whales is very lively."

"Out for now," said Genright. "I'm starved."

They sailed south following the herds, slowly, yet busily, sticking to their work schedules, accumulating data, transmitting reports, frequently checking in with Herd Base to say hello.

They were in old Tropic of Cancer waters abounding with life: bony fishes in abundance, squid, always the ambling whales, often seals and sea lions adventuring in open seas, or sea otters tired of the coast. They took to the water often in silco-membrane suits, sometimes with only tanks and fins. They sampled plankton species from oceanic prairies of the stuff that sustained the baleen whales and a thousand other life forms feeding at the bottom of the eternal food chain of the oceans.

They were in the sea working about two

weeks after Tube Steak and Tube Two had declined meeting the white shark when the pair of old bulls reappeared before them like instant islands and snorted limp blowhole greetings. Tube Steak drifted to where the work subs were tethered and buoyed and nudged them gently as though examining pups in a whale nursery before he turned again to face the swimmers.

"Greetings," said Tuktu.

"And hello again," added Toby Lee, paddling toward a fixed whale eye.

"Big hypos and brushes," said Kim.

"Back in a minute," Genright bubbled as he streaked for the divers' hatch of one of the subs.

Tube Two watched him go with bored, if perceptible, curiosity, then lowered his center of gravity so the sea could cool his back from the sun, and, from all appearances, dozed off awash.

"Just how am I supposed to climb up on you, you monster?" asked Toby, speaking into the eye. She surged toward Tube Steak's balancing pectoral sweep and pushed down upon it. As though asked prettily, Tube Steak sank lower into the sea. As Toby, Kim, and Tuktu swam over his back, he rose again, leaving them on the expansive skin-patio of his back.

"You think he knows what I said to him?" asked Toby suspiciously.

"Training," said Kim.

"He wants his back rubbed, that's all," Tuktu snorted. "And here comes Warden Three, Low Grade."

Genright was riding a portable sled, or rather being towed by it, because the sled was laden with canisters of dye, some oversized hypodermic needles that looked like syringes, and a collection of paint brushes.

He cruised in to dock beside Tube Steak and hurled some of his cargo to the waiting hydronauts.

"Color him gorgeous, he's mine. How do I get up there? Not enough barnacles for a handhold on this side."

"Knock on a pectoral and ask old TS nicely."

"You kidding me, buddy, square-shaped buddy?"

"Stay wet then, dolt."

Genright swam gingerly to the whale's flipper.

"May I board, sir?"

Tube Steak obliged.

"You've been teaching my whale tricks behind my back," Genright accused the others when he joined them. "I do the work around here. You play the funnies."

"Work now," ordered Kim.

The blubber of all cetaceans is fatty tissue in

which cells full of oil drops are bound together by tough, fibrous tissue. It is not soft or like pudding. It is hard, firm, and compact. It may vary from an inch in thickness in porpoises to more than a foot in the large rorquals such as the blue whales, and even more than that in sperm and right whales.

Blubber is an insulating layer to prevent the loss of heat from the warm body inside to the cold water outside. But whales exercise as violently as land animals, and their body heat rises with such exertion. They cannot sweat or pant to get rid of excess heat like land animals. So blubber is traversed by many blood vessels which bring the blood close to the surface of the skin for cooling. The flow through these blood vessels is controlled automatically by their muscular skin coats, thus regulating temperatures when the blubber layer keeps too much heat in the body.

"I think we stick the hypos in about an inch and inject the dye just around the stern area," said Kim. "It ought to color the skin internally. Then we smear the dye on the outside for luck, and hope it doesn't wear off in the traffic. The combination of methods ought to get us a bright yellow whale."

"We ought to divide and work on Tube Two

at the same time," suggested Tuktu. "He may get bored if we coddle his friend and ignore him."

"Sing to him. Play with his fins, and make him go up and down, bouncy, bouncy then, old square buddy. None of you would have any whales to play with if it weren't for me, you know."

"Stow it," snapped Kim.

It took the hydronauts a half-hour to adorn the two docile bulls. The great creatures seemed to enjoy the attention. Fortunately they couldn't see themselves. Science has not detected any particular sense of vanity among cetaceans, but creatures of the same species do better when they look like their peers. Tube Steak and Tube Two did not, as presently painted.

Two thirds of their great bodies were mottled black and gray, with the wrinkled hide scarred by time and environmental wounds. The stern third, with the exception of their restless flukes, bloomed against the blue sea like daffodils pictured in the hive city picture books.

The hydronauts, for once as gleeful as their years, were pleased with their efforts.

"I love them," cooed Toby Lee.

"Oh, so vast and so vastly improved," sang Kim.

Tuktu beamed, and Genright danced on Tube Two's slippery back.

Apparently annoyed by such hilarity, TT sank and moved off, and a moment later TS joined him, leaving the laughing artists swimming.

"Back to the boats," said Kim. "I want to see if they show in color on the sensing equipment. Think I ought to check in with Herd Base, too. Don't forget the sled."

Sometime later, dried, comfortable in boat fatigues or scrap clothing, and seated at the com console of *Adam 1*, Kim and Toby Lee had no difficulty in picking up the redone whales. They were not very far away anyhow. Each of them was scooping furrows of lunch from the bottom in about ninety feet of water.

"In deeper water our lights will make them glow," Kim said thoughtfully.

"You want Herd Base?"

"Yes."

"Have you *Adam One*," said the silky tones of Herd Command. "Any trouble?"

"We just dyed some of your whales," said Kim.

"You mean you killed some of our herds?"

"No. Dyed. As in color. Those two bulls I mentioned before."

"It was one, wasn't it?"

"Two now. Well, they are bright yellow in the stern sections now. Thought you ought to know in case some of your people expressed surprise."

"You asked permission to dye them?"

"Should we have?"

There was a long sigh. "Probably not. It would have been denied. Part of your work, I suppose?"

"Yes, sir."

"Instant identification. That sort of thing?"

"Yes, sir."

"We'll so record it and pass along the word. And speaking of dyed whales, as sort of a joke, of course. About twenty miles south of you is one of our processing plants, a sea-bed complex where we convert the live stock into end products for the cities. You and your teammates might want to visit it. Come in from the south. There's in-bubble docking for both your boats, and surface atmosphere so you won't need breathing gear. Just call Factory Six when you decide to visit and let 'em know when to expect you. Can't miss the place. There's a half-mile of it along the bottom at about five hundred feet."

"Thank you, sir."

"I'll alert the troops to watch over the yellow fellows. And one more word. You'll be in the birthing shallows soon. Lots of mating as well as touchy cows dropping young. Do nothing there abnormal. Move quietly. Observe. But, I emphasize, do not innovate anything no matter how special your assignment may be. Do you read?"

"Yes, sir."

The days spun by in the routines of their instructions: sediment studies seeking radioactive wastes of the old war, plankton analysis for future cultures, census of the animal life about them, mapping of sea changes by comparison with the old charts, temperature studies and thermocline readings, interminable probings with the sensing equipment. But always they watched the whales.

They saw cows calve in glassine shallows and the new babies nurse. Often they saw the autopods controlled by the herdsmen butt the young aside to attach and electronically suckle the cows for milk for the cities, taking only pre-set quotas so that the babies never went hungry. The autopods looked surprisingly like baby whales. The hydronauts doubted whether the whale mothers ever knew the difference between them and their own young.

They saw the young bulls frolic and breach for sport, heaving their tons into the air seemingly for pure muscular joy. They watched matings and sporadic herd fights.

Occasionally they saw giant splashes of primrose glint under an equally yellow sun, and knew that Tube Steak and Tube Two were in the vicinity. And once in a while the two bulls nosed by for a visit.

They did call at Factory Six, in essence and purpose a whaling factory much like those described in the ancient history tapes, but, in operation, a sterile, ruthlessly efficient process which gave instant death to selected stock and then reduced that stock to a maximum variety of components for use by the burrow cities. These components—meat, oils, bones, organic chemicals—entered great compressed-air viaducts and were shunted, station by station, to the coast for shipment, mostly by airpod freight shuttles jetted into missile flight for a distant hive.

The four young wardens stayed lean and muscle-tight by exercise in the boats and much swimming. Kim spent much time, some of it with Toby Lee's help, in tinkering with the sonic equipment running up and down frequency ranges to that unbearable point where he could "hear" or not "hear" as Toby spoke, and he could "hear" sound that certainly Toby could not detect as time went by. Toby Lee spent much time reading the Bible, and, surprisingly, so did Genright and Tuktu.

"It's a survival story," explained Tuktu, "a life pattern designed for a harsh land with codes and conducts to match."

"More, much more than that," added Toby Lee and Genright.

"It's a why for being, if you read it right, an affirmation of life that goes far beyond mere existence. It's sort of a simple master plan for mankind that makes every individual count as an individual, not as a number or a work unit in a group or, let's say, a city dweller," said Genright.

"It's a love story," added Toby Lee.

"A what story?" asked Kim.

"Well, nothing taught in our conditioning programs," snapped Toby, "but you are closer to that *what* story than you think, *I* think."

At night when the ocean was pond still, its darkness broken by light pools of fluorescence, the hydronauts sometimes broke out inflatable rafts just wide enough for two, tethered them to the work subs, and floated, wide-eyed, looking at the stars. They took hand lasers against prowling sharks, and lights to attract swarms of small fish to the surface for a change in diet when the mood took them.

Kim and Toby Lee, hand in hand and warmed by each other, never knew that some of the stars they watched had once been made by man at his technical best to lift the species beyond earth into the mysteries of space. The men who had created them were lost in time, but the machines they wrought still moved in forgotten orbits reflecting earth light, moonglow, and the space-bent rays of the sun. And some of those machines still contained the ancients who made and controlled them, frozen forever as they once were by the airless cold of space.

Much of their science endured in the histories and retrieval banks of the cities. Nuclear war and the instability of metals caused by radiation, even unknown gaps in the mathematics of the past, barred its use. Not until the earth was completely cleansed and its surface again explored and made habitable could the recycling of civilizations make star travel a hope once more.

The burrow cities and the seas were the present, and unsparing discipline and control of humanity, the reality.

One night as the hydronauts enjoyed the rafts, a glint of moonlight picked out two distinct patches of yellow about a half-mile away across the flat sea.

Genright spotted them first.

"Twelve o'clock due west," he said. "There's the tubes."

The silhouettes were plain and the yellow vivid as they stared over the open water. The color seemed to flicker like an arctic aurora as the whales drifted through the cold green patches of washed light generated by billions of micro-organisms.

"Tell me I'm wrong," shouted Genright, "but isn't there something moving with those bulls? Even a figure on one of their backs?"

"Not sure, but I think so," cried Tuktu.

Kim wasted no time looking harder. He rolled off the raft and swam for *Adam 1* and its sensing console. He popped through the sub's bottom bubble and sloshed to his instruments.

Sonar, radar, the laser cameras on recording circuits, infrared detectors, thermal probes, and open sound pickups—all the customary sensors, and all of them working—picked up the whales plainly at this comparatively short range. Kim made certain that all recording and filing instruments were collecting data.

There was something moving around the old bulls. There were two somethings, four-legged somethings with short, strong swimmer's tails and webbed swimmer's paws clad in sleek, furred coats topped by round, whiskered heads and stubbed ears. They looked very much like sea otters but about three times the size of the normal members of that merry clan. And as Kim watched, one of them stood erect on one of the whale backs and moved awkwardly, but surely, in a walking motion.

As it did so, it turned and faced the work subs as though it watched the boats, which could have been barely visible, if at all, in the deceptive light across the open water.

Kim made small manual adjustments in the visual equipment, increasing magnification of the zoom lenses.

The whiskered face showed a clearly lipped, generous mouth with slightly protruding carnivore's teeth, a widespread nose, nostriled, certainly for air breathing. The face, although flat, held eyes protected by a bony-ridged forehead. The range was too far to catch expression, but Kim had a distinct impression that, at closer distance, those eyes would show intelligence, perhaps distinctly human intelligence.

On a hunch he set the boat's pulsar beams to frequency just above the waves of human hearing and sent the sound skipping across open water. As he did so, he adjusted the audio receivers for vocal reception, leaving the sonar detectors alone.

The figure on the whale seemed to stiffen. It lifted a forepaw and seemed to wave it. And as it did so, Kim "heard" again a "sound" above sound, an inner voice for a micron of time, and felt the illusion that the "voice" spoke his own language.

The otterlike creature dived. The whales sounded, and the work sub's instruments recorded their going until they vanished from scan range many miles away.

It made sense, thought Kim, his green eyes aglow with discovery. It made sense—some sense? —nonsense? No. Plain sense, common variety, to him.

He shared it with heads in the hatch moments later.

"Figure it this way," he said. "The lab wizards of Hive Hawaii, working against time because their city was doomed, created their first hatch working from vision and chemical genius, perhaps, as a blueprint, an experiment, for a human designed to live in the sea.

"Then, thinking things through the centuries of human heritage factors, they had to compromise. They thought of the land masses still remaining which might again sustain humanity one day. They had to come to an amphibian form, but an improved pelagic amphibian. It had to have more ties to the oceans, yet still be able to exist, if the need arose, to use the land, particularly land bordering the seas. Rocks, beaches, islands . . . watery lands that would be first cleansed from radiation and nukie damage. . . . And, again because time was a factor for them, they put their big bet on the second hatch, the amphibs . . . these otter-types or whatever we find them to be. The third hatch, our seababies, was a reach for the absolute, total sea form. Maybe they couldn't make it, but their creators had to try while they had time to try. We may never know.

"But my bet is on the second hatch."

"Only a guess," Toby Lee said softly.

"A hypothesis," said Tuktu.

"All I know is, I never saw an otter, a real one, standing on a whale's back. I never saw or heard of any seal, sea lion, walrus, otter, or manatee messing around with any whales. I know what I saw tonight even if I don't know what it was I saw," said Genright firmly.

"Well, what we saw, thought, didn't see, or guessed, is all on the sensing records in this boat. And I'm going to raise Baja Base and talk to our friendly brass before I report it officially. It's all going to sound mighty silly anyhow.

"Okay, back, pick up the gear out there, and

man the boats for conference. Ten minutes give you enough time?"

The three nodded. Toby smiled.

"Be right back, sir," she said.

7

They raised Baja on the Service wave length and got Commanders Torrance and Jensen.

"The sea boileth," said Kim.

"Be right back on the private band," said Jensen's voice. And they were, within seconds.

"We had a report on yellow whales," said

Commander Torrance. "Bit gaudy, don't you think?"

"No sir," answered Kim. "But that wasn't why we called."

He told his story crisply, adding, once more, his own theories, and those of his associates.

"Seems to settle the delphine ideas," said Commander Jensen, "as to the forms of the aliens, at least."

"Advice, please, sirs. Do we try to contact Commander Brent through the regular report system or maybe raise the *Polaris* if he's using it for headquarters? Or do we just pass our observations along routinely as ordered? We do have records of tonight's visual contact with our whales."

"You what?" asked Commander Torrance.

"I thought I told you, sir, that I set all the sensing gear to record. As usual, I might add."

"Didn't get through to me, son. One moment. Want to think a bit with Jiggs."

"Jiggs, yet," said Genright.

"Heard that, Selsor. You say Jiggs, *sir*."

Toby Lee giggled.

"Hear this, Rockwell," said Commander Torrance. "You start north now from your position. It's about time for the herds to smell spring in the temperate zones and summer in the Arctic anyhow. Call us when you're off Baja, and we'll pick up your records for safekeeping. Meanwhile, we'll contact Commander Brent somewhat more privately than you can.

"After all, what you've put together will sound like crazy speculation to most Service personnel and, perhaps, others who might get the story, no matter what we think. Make that what *you* think. *We* don't know exactly what to think—"

"Although we think you're thinking straight," interrupted Commander Jensen. "It's just that we don't seem to believe in miracles, especially ones that haven't had time to happen."

"Oh, ye of little faith . . ." muttered Tuktu.

"Using the reading matter too, I gather," added Commander Torrance. "Anyhow, you have an order. Carry it out. And it's just possible that you might be hearing from Commander Brent directly."

"On our very own com system?" wailed Genright.

"Oh no," added Toby.

"Confidence in superiors is the keystone of the Service," Jiggs Jensen said serenely.

"I shall pass the word to my staff," Kim said brightly, if somewhat hollowly. "Good night, sirs."

"You are not dismissed. One caution. Should

any portion of your communications systems develop a need for repairs, I suggest you all find some haven in the Antarctic, preferably beneath the polar cap. Now, good night."

Commander Torrance was right about the herds. Even as the *Adams* headed north, there was a stirring among the grays as though some sense of awakening moved throughout the waters. All earthly animals own a biologic clock, the great cetaceans among them. Its alarm, usually triggered by light or perhaps seasons or fruiting glands, alters behavior patterns and changes the rhythms of animal life. Man too is subject to this clock, although man's own changes of his environmental influences make its workings erratic.

But in migrating beasts or birds, when the bell of the biologic clock clangs time to move, movement begins, and the cycle of another year turns onward.

By the time the hydronauts surfaced and hove to off Baja in the comparatively shallow waters, part of a sea buried height of bottom once mapped as a ridge bisecting the entire South Pacific Basin, the nursery waters had been evacuated by the whales.

The vanguard of the herds, mostly "teeny" males from age ten upward, and older bulls as well, were moving toward the northern summer and the chill seas of the North Pole. Still older males would be continually delayed by thumping, grunting fights, which, picked up by underwater sound detectors, were marked by odd gurgles and odder thumps that sounded like somebody banging sacks of wet sand with sledge hammers.

The herds, divided into squads, platoons, and companies, would move at an increased rate of speed as though already savoring the rich plankter meals off the Aleutians and in the Bering Sea, and the long arctic days where night made only brief courtesy calls.

Commanders Torrance and Jensen made the pickup of the records from *Adam I*. They arrived by jet-driven, A-powered surface boat about dusk. Kim cracked the seldom used top hatch to let them scramble aboard the gently bobbing work sub. *Adam II* was buoy-anchored nearby. Genright and Tuktu picked up the surface craft line and tethered it to the same buoy, then swam to *Adam I*. Kim kept pressure in the boat so the bottom bubble hatch could be opened and two heads could join the conference.

Jensen's huge frame dominated the interior of the boat, which suddenly seemed small with the addition of two more people.

"Whoosh," he said. "Such a small hole for such a big me, and me no longer young."

"We brought fresh steaks and fresh milk as our tickets," said Commander Torrance. "Abalone and whale respectively."

"Thank you, sir." Toby smiled. "Nice change."

"Enough for ten or twelve people?"

"Enough, Genright."

"Let's get to it," said Commander Torrance. "Tapes, video and plain sound tracks, recorder rolls, the works on both your theory, which, I trust, is explained, and that which you saw. You do have stuff on your duties as whale valets?"

"Include the record of my heroism in chasing the shark away," said Genright.

Tuktu grinned. "All it shows is you hiding behind a whale."

"No time. No time," snapped Commander Torrance. "Play later, if you wish. This is official business." He paused to gather complete attention.

"You will proceed as originally ordered, and as observers only, doing your daily work, making your usual reports. Commander Brent will get this material directly and not through channels. I am ordered to deliver it personally for his evaluation.

"Now he will have your closed com band,

which he promises not to monitor or violate in any way unless he intends to contact you directly and, I imagine, in total privacy at his end. I assume he does intend to make contact, perhaps from the *Polaris* or some fixed base.

"Now, and this is an order. I need not spell out the need for you to carry it out to the letter. You are not to initiate contact with your otter-people, sea men, merfolk, or any other suspects you may turn up. You are not, repeat, not, to make first moves. Should you be contacted or otherwise directly approached, use your best judgment as to procedure.

"That's it. Now make your second guesses or whatever you have in mind, and we'll guess along with you."

"Why doesn't he want us to make any first moves? Certainly that's the best way to show friendship and good intentions?" ventured Toby Lee.

"Because the Service doesn't know yet whether or not the Council wants to be friends," snapped Kim.

"Seems reasonable," said Commander Jensen.

"May be that, in view of Warden Petrie Putnam's big mouth, we aren't trusted," suggested Tuktu.

"Afraid we'll recruit our own Service," said Genright, grinning.

"Seems reasonable," Jiggs Jensen said placidly.

The hydronauts looked at the commanders with suspicion.

"Sirs, you aren't making any guesses at all," said Kim.

"We've made a few, Rockwell." Commander Torrance's voice was level.

"First, you must know that this entire search involves many people and much equipment in many places no matter how quietly it is conducted. Should Commander Brent find your reports and your records credible, he would need time to clue in many people about what sort of life form to focus upon, or suggest such a focus without giving a reason for it.

"We can safely guess that he has more problems than we can know about and he doesn't want the young to slam-bang into any alien contact until he resolves some of those problems. Particularly when you are already a part of them.

"As to trust, you heard your orders. You are trusted to use your own judgment if the sea strangers contact you first. It is assumed that you would report such contact immediately. That's trust. It is also faith in the fact that you know your own obligations to duty."

There was a long pause.

"We're off," said Commander Jensen, "and without that nice hot cup of something you were about to offer."

"Can't be away from base too long," added Commander Torrance. "Not even as messenger boys. Good luck, wardens. And no matter what the distances, stay in touch."

Kim waved Genright and Tuktu out of the bubble hatch, closed it, and dogged it tightly. He cracked the top hatch to let the commanders disembark for their own boat, and moments later, watched it slide into the dark for shore on the vision screen of the com console. He was restless tonight for no reason he could name as he took *Adam 1* down below possible surface turbulence and put her on a slow course northward. He could feel Toby Lee's eyes upon him and turned to meet them.

They were warm and speculative and questioning. She smiled slowly, kicked off her static-free felt slippers, and padded to him barefooted. She put her hands on his upper arms. Still seated, he leaned and rested his forehead on her chin.

"Back to the search, sir," she said.

He cut the constant boat lights from automatic and dimmed them manually, leaving only the com console and the instruments glowing.

"Man has to look," he muttered.

"Woman too."

"It's duty." He grinned, and a tiny giggle wove around his chuckle.

The grays were not the only whales moving north as the days passed and the seas greened and grew more chill above thirty degrees latitude. Groups and families of sperm whales were also about their migratory journeys.

The size of these giants among the toothed whales with their box-square heads and armed lower jaws awed the hydronauts. If the mutated grays were immense, the sperms were titanic. Many of the males bound for arctic waters leaving their females and young to rove the warmer depths of lower latitudes were over ninety feet. When they blew stale air and often spray from their single nostril, the jet stood firm as a geyser before the winds reduced it to a thousand droplets.

The sperm males were wary as the work boats tried to approach them closely. A few were aggressive. They were meat eaters, after all. The hydronauts discouraged them with the pulsars set to nagging low frequencies which they seemed to find unpleasant.

The hydronauts soon noticed that from time to time single males would vanish for as much as two hours on feeding forays or other mysterious errands into the depths.

One day they followed a prime bull as he slanted from the surface on a seemingly random course into the depths. Moving silently as shadows under the thermocline through the light zones of green and indigo dusks into total blackness, with the sensing equipment tracking the huge sperm whose own sonar clacking was also scanning the depths, they moved steadily deeper. Only streaks of light from luminescent fishes and formless creatures occasionally made exclamation marks in the blackness.

The pressure against the impervious hulls of the work subs measured more than a hundred tons to the square foot.

Simultaneously the sensing systems of the boats and the sonar of the whale picked up another giant object. The sperm had found its prey, a monstrous squid, some seventy feet of arms and tentacles with gripping, "suction cups," with a huge mouth and a razor-edged, parrotlike beak. And it charged to meet it with jaws agape to fix its sixty lower jaw teeth into the rubbery central body of the squid.

Kim ordered lights, which splintered the darkness and bathed the rending battle in a weird glow. Boat cameras picked up the desperate clutching of tentacles trying for a grip on the sperm's boxlike head and the beak chipping chunks of flesh from the whale's hide, now oozing blood.

The fight went on for nearly ten minutes in a froth of heaving bodies. Then the great slab of lower jaw clanged shut in a final grip on the squid's head, crushing out its life, and leaving its tentacles streaming limp and without direction. They fluttered like pennants of a lost cause as the whale drove for the surface, carrying a giant meal for a hungry warrior.

The hydronauts watched as the whale allowed the carcass to drift and began to breathe as though it intended to consume the sky. It exhaled in a jet of vapor, a blend of stale air and what appeared to be a grayish foam that clung to its head in patches. The sperm inhaled and blew without stopping for minutes, paying the oxygen debt to its great body that it had borrowed from its lungs and tissues in the deep. Then it began to feed, shearing off chunks of squid, which it shoveled down its gullet with its tongue until all that remained of the cephalopod was fleshy rubble for smaller fish. Even the indigestible horny beak vanished.

"You realize that fellow went down almost four thousand feet to pick up that snack?" asked

Genright on the intercom. "Think of that pressure, and holding his breath for over an hour—"

"And his only equipment was him," added Tuktu.

"We know how he does it, but just *how* does he do it?" whispered Toby Lee.

Man in the sea carries an outside air supply with him, compressed and sometimes mixed with helium, for work in the depths. The air pressure within his diving suit is always greater than the pressure of the water outside it. There is no difficulty in breathing compressed air. Trouble comes when the diver ascends and pressure is eased. During the dive the nitrogen in compressed air dissolves in the blood and body tissues to the saturation limit for the pressure without bothering man. But when he comes up, the nitrogen comes out of solution more quickly than he can get rid of it through his lungs. It forms bubbles in his blood vessels, which stop the blood flow and cause a gas embolism that can be fatal. Even when the gas bubbles do not produce an embolism they cause extreme pain once known as "the bends." And the only cure is for the diver to be recompressed and for the pressure to be released gradually, usually in a decompression chamber. It is a long process.

Deep divers like the great sperms withstand

great depth pressures, but they never get the bends. The difference between man and whales is that the human takes an unlimited supply of air with him so that nitrogen can dissolve in the blood to the limit of saturation. The whales take only the air contained in their lungs and air passages. Their supply is limited, so, consequently, there is little or no nitrogen to dissolve in their blood.

As to pressure, when a sperm dives, for instance, the water pressure, or hydrostatic pressure, is transmitted to all parts of its body. But the animal's body consists of 90 per cent water, and since water is nearly incompressible, its body is not squashed or deformed.

The air in its lungs is compressible, however. With increasing depths the lungs become more and more collapsed and its air is forced into the windpipe and passages to the blowhole, which are not as well supplied with blood vessels as the lungs. Thus gas exchange from the air to the tissues is reduced.

Whales own safeguards against drowning and the bends. The passage from windpipe to blowhole is a twisting, winding one. It is connected with side passages and with air sacs related to the under parts of the skull. The sacs are filled with foam, an emulsion of water, oil, and air, and the oil absorbs nitrogen.

The head of the sperm whale, which comprises nearly a third of its body, holds much oil and a waxy-solid called spermaceti, which may also absorb nitrogen.

The twisting, winding passageway leading to the blowhole (spiracle) also acts as a valve to prevent the escape of air or the entrance of water during a dive. When a sperm opens his huge mouth to seize food in the depths, water cannot get into its lungs.

The upper end of the windpipe is firmly held by the inner end of the blowhole pipe or internal nostrils into which it projects. The valve system is perfect.

The days lengthened as *Adams I* and *II* cruised ever northward. The grays began a westward sweep, keeping an erratic pace which sometimes logged many miles each day and very few on other days, depending upon the richness of the feeding grounds. They raised and swept along the great sickle-shaped chain of the Aleutian Islands, born in volcanic action and still being altered by it. The hydronauts could see coned peaks that were capped in smoke and flame rising as high as nine thousand feet into the sky, their snow fields splattered by ash and cinders.

Most of the islands etched sharp in the sensing instruments, were barren, cleansed by winds that never stopped blowing in any season, although some showed pastures of rank grasses. Many were homes to sea birds in a world bereft of most of its land flyers by the old wars. The identity tapes showed puffins, petrels which dipped continually into the sea for the same plankters which fed the whales, and cormorants.

Kim was alarmed by the seismic readings picked up by the work subs. If they were correct, the sea bed and the islands were made of nervous stuff which twitched in volcanic tremors and shiftings.

"I'd say this whole area could blow wide open at any time," he told Toby Lee.

"The whales don't show any fear," she said. "And I'm sure instinct would warn them of anything serious."

"Maybe," he said, "but just maybe."

They followed the whales through the wider passes of the islands as they picked their way into the Bering Sea, staying strictly away from the narrower straits where racing currents and tides turned the water into hissings of foam and treacherous rips.

Occasionally they left the *Adams* buoy-tied to explore, and to get what Kim never tired of explaining as "the feel of the sea." "If you haven't got it and can't get it, you don't belong in this business," he said solemnly to in-sea buddies that couldn't have agreed more.

They wore shield suits and went armed, protected by suit heating elements against water chill and the unexpected danger by weaponry. They watched porpoises feed on the small silver fish called "capelin." They saw bull fur seals cruising alone, perhaps headed for rocky islands where they would haul out for summer. They dived along undersea cliffs where rock cod hunted food in kelp forests, and they saw diving birds like the cormorants plumb the depths for smaller sizes of the same cod. They counted benthic species of crabs, slugs, snails, urchins. And now and then, they used the pulsar tubes or the handgun lasers to rout bigger predators who inspected the hydronauts.

Always they watched the whales, forever looking for those larger than sea otter, otter forms they had seen with their—somehow they felt like parents—gray bulls.

They had not seen Tube Steak and Tube Two for more than three weeks, no matter how hard they searched for a glimpse of yellow in the emerald waters or among the drifting floes of sun-chipped bergs.

"Maybe their bosses gave 'em orders to stay away from us," suggested Genright.

"If they were around, we'd have picked them up one way or another," said Tuktu.

"Maybe they've got a hideaway in these waters," murmured Toby Lee.

"Ummm," agreed Kim, "but they'll show."

They did—off the Pribilofs, shining like polished fruit and blowing limp fountains of greeting immediately in front of the surfaced subs.

"Tuktu, let's look 'em over," said Kim. "Toby and Genright, stay with the boats. Shield suits and tanks, assorted gear, in case they've forgotten their friends. Make it fast, eh?"

The grays had not forgotten. They were amiable as Tuktu and Kim swam around them. Tube Steak allowed his nose to be patted, and Tube Two even nudged Tuktu in a most gentle surge that sent the hydronaut washing ten feet below the surface with both arms and legs disorganized.

"They look awfully clean to me somehow," said Kim.

"You notice that?" he asked both boats.

"No growths," reported Toby.

"I'd say they've been in fresh water for a time to get that scrubbed look," added Genright.

"I'm going up for a better look," said Kim,

swimming close to Tube Steak and pushing against his huge pectoral.

The gray accommodated him by settling while he swam across its back and knelt while TS rose again.

"Whoosh," he said. "Mighty slippery, and his skin looks fresh and new as it can get with all those old scars. You don't suppose these animals have had a hot bath?"

"They're fatter too," contributed Tuktu. "At least, I think so. Maybe shore duty? Rest and recreation leave?"

The whales drifted over and touched heads with the boats.

"You think they're trying to tell us something?" asked Toby.

"We're coming in," said Kim suddenly, and slid off TS's back into the sea.

He closed the bubble hatch and dogged it tightly behind him as he entered the boat and stripped off his gear, which he exchanged for scant work shorts before joining Toby at the instrument console.

The whales were circling both *Adams* tightly as if waiting for Kim and Tuktu to rejoin the boats and ready them for movement. Then they moved off, circling once more as though rounding up the subs, and set out, south, for the Aleutians.

"I'd say they wanted to be followed," murmured Tuktu over the com system.

"Well, why not?" asked Kim. "Let's go."

The whales swam resolutely, pausing only to feed, and the boats dawdled in their wake, continually observing the waters. As though antiseason, the bulls went south, slanting through Bering waters that averaged little more than one hundred feet in depth. They crossed the island chain and swam east on the surface of the four-thousand-foot waters which the old charts once showed as the Aleutian Trench. They veered east close to the land mass, and there they slowed for a few days to feed, almost aimlessly.

The hydronauts went about their daily routines.

One day a huge berg shining like a great blue-green jewel towered into view, a slice of crystal ice sheared from some monstrous glacier. It glistened with surface moisture, its compressed hardness nearly impervious to sun. The *Adams* surfaced and cruised around it, wary of any unseen extrusions at its base.

And as the sensing gear sent visual probes into its transparent interior, the hydronauts saw an amazing tableau. Frozen in the glacier were two adults, a man and a woman, holding hands with a child between them. The tiny group stood erect, faces lifted toward some ancient sky, their bodies poised defiantly.

There was a strange peace on those faces, even small smiles at the corners of the mouths. The eyes were wide open, the man's blue, the woman's blue, and the child's, a girl, green.

The man was blond and fair. He looked amazingly like Kim. All of the group were clad in some sort of uniform, skirted for the females. But all were lightly clad as though they were locked in an eternal summer preserved forever in the ice.

"Cryos," said Tuktu.

"I don't think so," said Kim. "Or at least, not deliberate Cryos placed there for posterity by some government for the future to revive and use again."

"I've never seen anything like them on the history scanners," added Toby Lee.

"Maybe they're older than our histories, way older," muttered Genright.

"White people, Caucasian, and probably out of place."

"Out of time too . . . time lost, Kim," said Toby.

"Decisions, decisions. Do we follow our whales or report the Cryos and stay with them until something arrives to pick them up?"

"Report first," said Tuktu.

"Wait until we get an order," flipped Genright.

"Well, we can mark the berg, then report and go on," said Kim.

"TS and TT aren't in any hurry," noted Toby.

They reported—and almost immediately received another surprise. They raised the *Polaris*. They raised Commander Brent. His voice was crisp. It was also formal.

"Thank you for the report, Rockwell, and wardens. Stand by. I shall be back to you immediately."

"But not on open band length I'll bet," muttered Kim.

He was right. Their private communications system winked alert, and Commander Brent's voice entered both work subs.

"The *Polaris* will pick up the Cryos, and within approximately forty-eight hours. We are not far from you at our speed range, and the work is delicate. Meanwhile, you will surface, and I assume you have, and transmit camera readings using both infrared and normal scanning processes to the *Polaris* on these settings."

The Commander gave them.

"Now listen carefully. I don't have much time. You know of the Putnam report of that business at Baja. It is still in my custody, but there is a chance that it will be reopened as a matter of routine rechecking, and you will be ordered back to Olympia Base until the matter is disposed. Commanders Torrance and Jensen have also been notified. It could be a little sticky, but unless something untoward happens, I don't anticipate too much trouble.

"I have passed the word concerning your otter-people, and the search is focusing upon them. I commend you for your records and your thinking about them, although I suggest that the subject is still highly speculative.

"The *Polaris* is in these waters because this is sea otter and amphibious mammal country in general.

"I am taking you into my complete confidence, perhaps foolishly, but I am now convinced for reasons of my own that should we locate the so-called Hawaiian second hatch we shall be ordered by the Council of Cities to destroy as much of it as we can find."

There was silence in *Adam I,* an equal hush in *Adam II.*

Commander Brent's even voice went on:

"You disregarded similar orders once before in the case of the sea babies. I disapproved at the time despite my personal feelings. You got away with your action. While not all of the Council knows all of the reasons for our current mission, I can tell you that those of it who do know are resolute men dedicated only to the survival of the hive cities and the status quo.

"You now stand in danger of disrepute or worse should the Putnam report result in hearings. I need not remind you of consequences should we find the new race and you disregard orders concerning it."

"Blessed are the peacemakers," muttered Genright.

"The literature from which you quote is classified and decreed officially lost," continued Commander Brent.

"You seem familiar with it, sir," added Toby Lee firmly.

"I am indeed. But again, my time is short. I have your information on the reappearance of your two grays and their condition. That condition suggests drastically altered environment, changed waters. I don't pretend to understand you young, but I gather from your information that you seem to think those whales want you to follow them?"

"We didn't say as much, sir," answered Kim.

"Then let us say I read more into the transmittal than you actually said, and correctly."

"Yes, sir."

"Were that not true, I should order you out of your present position. Again because I have taken you into my complete confidence, you should know that I may be risking your lives because of my own curiosity, and telling myself I am risking your safety because of the success of the mission.

"The *Polaris* carries instruments denied your work subs. Your own sensors have doubtless recorded seismic disturbances, and right now, your temperature gauges show a reading of some two degrees above what your sea heat should be if normal."

"We are in comparatively shallow ocean, sir," said Kim.

"The berg that holds the Cryos is sweating, isn't it?"

"The sun is warmish, sir."

"None the less, Rockwell, what the *Polaris* probes indicate is sea-bed heat and tremors too fine for your sensors to read. You are in a most unstable volcanic area with a long history of unpredictable violence, and we are reading the first faint signs of possible disruptions. By the time your own instruments, good as they are, confirmed and recorded such signs, you could be in big trouble."

"Would the whales know that, sir?"

"The Service does not yet know all there is to know about the power of instinct. Nor, I might add, do those responsible for our own life conditioning and our imposed psychic patterns know either."

"Treason," muttered Genright.

"Isn't it?" remarked Commander Brent, and his voice scarcely concealed his broken-twig chuckle.

"But mark your berg for the *Polaris*, and follow the bulls. Further, this is an order. Leave both your Service communications and your own private com system open until I contact you personally or, perhaps, Commanders Torrance and Jensen. Just remember that both frequencies may be heard, your own by me or persons I can trust completely. Out."

8

"All hands rig for in-boat wigwag," said Genright.

"All hands rig for in-boat lip reading," muttered Toby Lee.

"Tuktu, jab a pennant in that berg or give it a splash of dye," ordered Kim. "Our guides look about ready to move. We'll go with them, and you and Genright follow when ready."

"Aye, aye, sir," answered Tuktu.

"You should see what signs he's making with his hands," said Genright.

The whales moved northeast on the south side of the island chain through seas with an odd, oily sheen that seemed to struggle to lift waves suddenly weighted. They moved steadily and at a good pace, their yellow sterns bright in the long daylight still strong in a waning afternoon. They continued to move well into bright nightfall until they paused for rest and a feeding session amid pastures of rich plankton.

The hydronauts altered their schedules to keep the bulls always in sensor sight. And with Commander Brent's warning in mind, they checked and rechecked instruments for bottom shocks, alien sounds which could not be attributed to animal life, and always for temperature changes.

The cetaceans swam again before daybreak in a sea streaked with dawn mist. They were oddly alone in waters that should have belonged to king salmon, cod, hair seals, and other swimmers both fish and mammals.

The *Adams* followed steadily at slow boat speed for a work sub. They crossed the midnight depths of the Aleutian trench again, and recrossed it once more to shallow water. Near noon the whales led them around a headland and along a mountainy mass of shore line.

Heavy mist hung on that shore line, the top of its curtain roiled by some wind pouring from a land height. The scanners, penetrating the fog, showed stretches of rocky, cliff-girt beaches and heavy surf.

The whales fluked toward a break in the beach line, and then halted.

"Water temp is up and rising here," said Tuktu.

"I mean it's up," added Genright.

"Confirmed," said Toby Lee.

"I'm going to topside and crack a hatch," said Kim. "I want to smell that mist for a second or two and eyeball that land person to person."

"Feel of the sea and all that, right?"

"You couldn't be righter, Tuktu."

"While you smell we'll run a bottom sample or two. The two tubes seem to be on station."

"I was thinking the same thing," said Toby.

The air smelled like cooking chowder, rich and burnt, yet savory with weed spices. It owned an alien warmth that seemed like a blandishment from a misplaced tropic current. The cliffs above the beach line, visible over the mist, were black, showing color only where the high sun lapped them.

Kim closed the hatch, dogged it, and ran an expert eye over its inner fittings to make certain all seals were tight to maintain the integrity of the inner, pressure hull. He had the funny feeling that *Adam I*, new and sturdy as she was, might be asked to stand strain. Unconsciously he squared his shoulders.

Toby Lee looked at him, and again, as many times before, he felt their oneness.

"Something?" she asked softly.

"Something," he nodded. "The whales?"

"Fidgety, I'd say."

He walked to the com console and raised *Adam II*. "Everything all right there?"

"Except the feel of this place," Tuktu's deep voice answered calmly.

"Whales have company," said Genright.

The otter forms were back. Toby Lee counted ten of them. They swarmed over the whales, and one of them stood erect and waved at the work subs, his fur coat gleaming in a sun growth suddenly dimmer as they watched.

"Report," said Kim. "Time, place, navigation fix, instrument readings. Call *Polaris* direct as well as the open band monitors which are already picking us up. I'm going to try to answer contact. Note I said answer, not initiate. We've already been waved at, and I call that a direct signal. I'm taking our transmittal up the frequency range, way up, as I speak."

The private com boomed a command.

"Rockwell," said Commander Brent's voice. "Get those boats away from that coast and into a southwest heading for open sea as fast as you can."

"Sir," said Kim, "we have been contacted by objects of our search. I am trying to make that contact a two-way one. *Adam Two* is now sending a complete report."

He could hear Tuktu's voice on both bands and knew that all sensing equipment capable of transmission was at work.

Commander Brent's voice snapped into both subs like a living presence.

"Leave the area at once!"

The sea heaved. It exhaled steam, and it tossed both work subs completely out of the water with a stunning shock that was followed by an impact of re-entry that spilled both Kim and Toby Lee against the bunk bulkheads.

They struggled erect and tilted to the com and instrument console, which, despite the blow on the hull, was still functioning. Their viewers showed a section of cliff sliding into the wall of surf, wiping out the beach before it.

Tube Two lay belly up in a foaming wash, its

body bent into an obviously fatal angle. Tube Steak seemed inert but unharmed. One of the otter-people swam groggily. The others had vanished into the steam which blanketed the humping swells.

Genright's voice filled *Adam I*.

"We're breaking up, Kim, but Tuktu and I are all right. There's a big crack across the weldglass in the stern, and we think that end of the boat is about to snap off. Tuktu's loading a sled with gear —shield suits, weapons, communications stuff. We'll go out the bubble and try for a beach."

"We'll pick you up," Kim said steadily.

"Don't think there's time for the swim to you," continued Genright. "Water temp is up to high eighties and rising. That shock has a brother coming any time now if the instruments are right. It's a big bottom eruption and what Brent was giving orders about, so leave now. We couldn't find you visually from the water anyhow once we leave the boat."

"That otter is waving again," said Toby Lee.

The thin, piercing verge of sound pitch entered Kim's head from the all-band speaker which had ranged into the ultrahigh frequencies before the shock hit the boat. It hurt as it probed, but suddenly it made distinguishable words.

"Follow the whale," it said. "Hole under land. Take you to sea people and safety."

"That otter or whatever is hurt, and Tube Steak's moving," said Toby.

Somewhere below them, and traveling the contours of the ocean bed, was a low growling as though a titanic organ trembled before sounding a bass note.

"We're out and leaving," panted Genright's voice. "See you later. Luck."

Kim put *Adam 1* into a small surge of movement.

"We're going to pick up that otter," he said. "You take the boat. I'm going out the bubble for him. I heard him, Toby. He said to follow Tube Steak to a hole in the cliff."

"Don't go."

"No choice. We need him, and we can't do anything for Tuktu and Genright now."

"Stay with the boat till I tell you to go," said Toby.

The water was oily, and it reeked of a thousand sulphurous stinks as it laved Kim's body. The otterlike creature moved limply as Kim turned it to a back position in the water. There was clearly gratitude in its deep-set eyes as he began the tow back to *Adam 1*, where Toby Lee helped him move it gently into the boat.

They placed it on the deck.

"Get a blanket and stimulant from the big kit," ordered Kim. "I want a look at Tube Steak."

The great bull was moving off toward the shore line, and as Kim watched, it dived. *Adam I* followed.

As they made the descent Kim spoke into the instrument panel.

"Calling *Polaris. Calling Polaris* . . ." He gave his report, position fix, and requested the search for Tuktu and Genright. "Have sea person aboard, and at person's instruction am following gray whale to unknown tunnel through cliff. Am expecting new eruptions and seismic action momentarily. Make sure you get Tuktu and Genright. Out."

The whale headed for what was apparently a fold in the sea bed, a V notched into rock which glowed a sullen red as *Adam I*'s light picked it up, and then leveled to find the flash of yellow that was Tube Steak. Depth readings measured three hundred feet as the V developed an overhang and became a black hole in the land face.

The big gray swam steadily as though impelled with some driving purpose, and *Adam I* surged in its wake.

The tunnel was a perfect circle cored smoothly through the rock as though cut by some machine. Kim sensed a strong current in the water flow which led him to think that *Adam 1*, if held to course, could make the passage without any power but that of the stream itself.

The passage went on and on, and ahead of the hydronauts the whale seemed to falter as it swam.

"This is a long dive for a gray," whispered Toby.

Then the core sloped upward. The streaked rock ended, and *Adam 1* entered a stretch of tunnel walled with ice. The lights became a glare, a crystal dazzle, and the walls turned deep green, electric blue, then clear as though no walls existed at all, and only the emerald jet of water sustained their movement.

Kim grunted, and a small whimper broke from Toby Lee's throat. For nearly a hundred yards on either side of *Adam 1*, locked deep within the embrace of the ice, were people like the prisoners they had seen in the floating berg. They were fair people, again in some uniform. There were, perhaps, fifty of them, some of them children, and the boat's sensing equipment picked them up and ticked them away in the visual data banks of the boat.

"A colony? Some shore detail? The personnel of a forgotten mission? What, Kim? What?"

"Maybe the people who made this tunnel," he guessed. "It doesn't seem to be a natural one."

Far behind them there was an echoing boom, followed nearly two minutes later by a sudden surge in the water around them which nearly slammed *Adam 1* into the ice walls.

Toby looked at Kim and shuddered.

"Closed?" she asked.

"Maybe," he said, and smiled suddenly. "We're still fine."

The tunnel widened and vanished.

The whale angled upward and surfaced.

And moments later, *Adam 1* bobbed upon still waters in daylight.

Kim cracked the top hatch, and fresh air spilled into the boat around them. They mounted the fold ladder and poked their heads into the sky.

They were in a lake, a crater so vast they could not see its far shore. They tilted their heads and saw a ring of remote peaks, mountains which humped so high that they found their own horizons, and the sun against their shoulders turned great snow fields a thousand hues of violet and crimson.

A quarter of a mile away Tube Steak heaved and blew and blew for new air.

Behind them, clustered by the hundreds on

rock platforms, many wet and shining, were the otter-people, the sea persons, all of them patiently watching *Adam 1* and the hydronauts.

"Let's see to our friend," said Kim.

9

"Is the sled all right?" groaned Tuktu. "The gear?"

"You don't care whether I'm all right or not?"

"I know you're all right. You're always all right, but then I also care. Where do you hurt?"

"Where do you?"

"Tell you later. Now we think and fast. This

place might not be here much longer. Us either if everything boils over with bumps and slides."

They lay on a thin strand of rocky beach which ended in a sheer cliff face. The sled, pulled out of water beside them, was intact, its lashings tight. They were in shield suits, donned to protect them against the rising water temperatures when they left the stricken *Adam II*. They checked them carefully: tanks, okay; all band communicators, okay; holstered pulsars, laser tubes, pellet ejectors for anesthetic use, miniature nerve gas globules or the capsules designed for internal explosion within large predators.

They gazed out over the steaming waters trying to see some familiar forms in the mist.

"Well," said Genright thoughtfully. "Unless the bottom opens and swallows her, we know *Adam II*'s out there in nothing more than a hundred and fifty to two hundred feet. We sprayed the com console and the recording banks with protective gel, so she ought to be salvageable later—"

"Unless that half-a-bean unit of A power cracked out of its shielding enclosure and spilled radiation poison that'll be around for the next five hundred years."

"Don't be gloomy, Tuktu."

"I won't be gloomy. I would rather be off."

"Where?"

"Hmmmmm . . ."

"You think the *Polaris* will be in here?"

"We heard all the gabble Kim sent about locations and fixes. We also heard all Toby's chatter during his rescue of that otter-man. We know about following the whale into the tunnel. And if we know all that, the *Polaris* knows it too, and Commander Brent will be along if possible. I don't think he'll be friendly when he comes."

"What did we do?"

"Genright, old buddy, study it. It isn't what we did, it's what we didn't. We didn't leave the area as ordered. And we didn't exactly refrain from contact with the new friends."

"Fella waved at Kim, you know."

"I heard. Some big initial contact. Commander Brent and others heard too."

"Well, we couldn't have gotten out anyhow."

The beach shuddered as Genright spoke. Then it rippled noticeably.

"I've got a notion we'd be better off in the water," said Tuktu.

"Agree. Maybe less shock, and take our chances with heat. Did I tell you I'm scared?"

"How could you be? I'm here, and all this clammy sweat on my forehead is from pure courage."

"Trust the Service, they taught us. I'm going to try for the *Polaris*."

"Make it fast then."

Their heads vanished into masks and helmets and the built-in com units within them.

They raised the *Polaris* first try, and with it Commander Brent's dry-ice voice demanding a location.

"It will be some time before we can reach you. Can you stay where you are?"

The beach rippled again, and a faint, burning musk odor blended with the swirling mist.

"Assume part of *Adam II* might be habitable?" asked Commander Brent.

"It's bottomed, sir," said Tuktu, "and we don't want to be on that bottom right now. It may be fissuring. We know it's doing something. The beach is sort of crawling under us. And the cliff behind us may let go on our heads. We're thinking about entering the water for whatever cushion value it might have."

There was a brief silence, then Commander Jensen's voice, soft and somehow merry, reached them.

"Assume you heroes saved enough survival gear from the work sub you smashed up? How did you break your toy, Genright? It was designed for everlasting life, you know."

"Tuktu and I were just rasslin' around a bit. Good to hear you, Jiggs, sir. How soon can you be here?"

"No hurry, heroes," snapped Commander Torrance's voice. "You're going to be put under charges anyhow, and if Rockwell ever comes within reach he'll be rescrambled until only his basic genes will remain for reassembly. That cheer you up? Make you forget your troubles?"

"It sure helps," laughed Tuktu. "All you brass holding a meeting?"

"No," said Commander Brent, suddenly gentle, "just sitting around chuckling and reading the instruments."

A great hollow boom assailed the hydronauts. A half-mile distant, the mist was blown away by some monstrous explosion, and the sea on the edge of a strip of washed shale rose into a towering geyser. The earth had blown seemingly as the whales blow when they surface from the depths.

"There's a hole down there," said Genright.

Tuktu spoke almost drowsily. "You thinking what I'm thinking?"

"The tunnel?"

"We can't make it here. We've got to try."

"That blast may have busted it closed."

"We try anyhow."

From far across the steam-hidden waters and

the miles of open sea, Commander Brent's voice, thin with interference, yet firm, said "God bless you, gentlemen wardens, and good luck."

"Luck and luck," echoed the voices of Commanders Torrance and Jensen.

The hydronauts swiveled the sled from the grip of the beach and entered the water. Adjusting their shield suits for diving, they let the sled tow them toward the site of the geyser.

The water was agitated. It was also warm and murky with suspended sediment. Their lights, thin-beamed though they were, seemed diffused. The sled, although buoyant, was sluggish as its water jets pushed it into the depths.

The current found the tunnel for them in the end. It literally streamed them toward the entrance or what was left of an entrance now nearly blocked with rocky debris.

"Never get a work sub through that hole now," said Tuktu.

"Let's hope it was through and found clear sailing all the way," added Genright.

"That muck could be cleaned out again easily enough. Beam it out with the lasers if we had to, and in no time."

"What we've got now is plenty of no time, buddy. The sled is just going to squeak through. And let's hurry before the bottom drops out of the bay or the top falls in with the next shock wave. I didn't like the way Commander Brent said they were sitting around reading the instruments. It didn't sound as though the *Polaris* was racing to our rescue."

"Who's going to race to pick up prisoners, especially baddies like us who disobey orders?"

The water was clearer inside the tunnel as the sled and the swift current swept them onward. The lights seemed brighter.

They were dumb-struck when they reached the ice walls and saw the entombed inhabitants. Those walls were flawed. Apparently a great seismic finger had pryed a section of the ice into the tunnel. Two blocks of glacier, one with a girl embedded within it, another a man, floated ahead of them.

"Nothing to say, Genright?"

"I'm adjusting to the trip."

"Keep adjusting. I think we're moving up a slope. We might be nearing the end of this road. You notice the water's colder?"

"I'm still too busy adjusting. And what I'm adjusting to most is what happens when we get to the exit. You suppose we'll be met?"

"You mean by Kim and Toby Lee?"

"I mean by a committee of otter-men, preferably friendly."

"I'll tell everybody you're a friend of mine and they'll like you right away."

The sled surfaced. They were in the great mountain-girdled lake. *Adam 1* bobbed before them. So did the huge blocks of ice, each with its silent passenger. And Toby Lee's voice was shouting:

"Hey, Tuktu and Genright, welcome aboard!"

They steered toward the work sub.

"You notice anything, Gen?"

"Nothin' special. Just a mob of overgrown sea otters."

"Men, buddy. Otter-humans. The second hatch at home."

"I'm adjusting."

"I've got a notion that all of us will be adjusting a long time, and right here."

"You don't think Commander Brent will find us?"

"I don't think he's going to look real hard. We and the New Breed are problems, and he needs thinking time. He'll expect us to contact him if we survive and are able."

"What do you mean if we survive?"

"You might catch a bad cold."

They left the sled tethered to *Adam 1* and scrambled to her sloped deck and the open hatch, where Toby Lee awaited them.

"Where's Kim?" they demanded.

"Ashore with a friend, I think. I don't know where. You want to tell me why you are here?"

"I think, you female," Genright said grandly, "that the answer to that is, we are here because there was not going to be a there at the other end of your tunnel."

"You want us to go find Kim?" asked Tuktu.

"He said to wait. He was explicit. I'm not worried yet. Besides, there may be another chore to do right here." She nodded toward the huge blocks of ice bobbing toward the middle of the lake, each carrying its eerie cargo.

"They'll keep for a long time," said Tuktu seriously, "and we ought to talk that matter over very carefully before we do anything. You know about Cryos, and we aren't high-ranking hive city psykes."

"Agree," nodded Genright. "We had one experience with Cryo Ury Kaane that none of us will ever forget. And anyhow, now that I am here, where's my whale?"

Toby shook her head at him as though in despair.

"You are too much." She waved at the vast expanse of water girdled about with the distant mountains. "He went that-a-way."

"Fine. I have plenty of time to eat before I summon him up."

"Now, my friend," said Kim, bending over the furred figure on the cabin deck of *Adam I*. "Let's see what we can do for you."

The eyes beneath the ridged brows and the hair-tufted cheekbones were warm and expressive. They even held a glint of humor.

Kim put his hands on the otter body gently, seeking broken bones and other injuries. He muttered as he worked.

"Good, good, good . . . Ah, not good. That shoulder now, and the foreleg. Shoulder may be dislocated, and the forepaw is broken. I can set it with a gel splint, which will be comfortable. Hold on now. This will give you pain."

He rotated the shoulder ever so gently, yet firmly, and heard it click into place.

"Toby Lee," he shouted. "Bring me the kit. I need a gel splint and a pain pill that won't make our friend feel sleepy."

"Coming," she said. "Why don't you ask me how I feel and examine me for injuries? Why don't you even hold me a little, you oaf?"

"I don't have to, Warden Three, I know all there is to know about your condition, just as you know all there is to know about mine. This fella saved our lives, I'm sure. And he's hurt."

Kim felt the high-frequency keening note, that sound above sound, for a brief moment. He looked down at his patient.

"You're talking," he said. "But you're going to have to come down the range for me much more before I can get it right."

He pointed to his ears and then the floor. He felt the ears of the otter-man and pointed to the ceiling.

The brown eyes stared at him, first puzzled, and then with a flicker of understanding, and finally with dawning intelligence. The creature raised its usable paw and with a muscular twitch, rolled back the fur from that paw to expose what appeared to be a hand.

The hand was webbed, a swimmer's utensil. And with it the otter-man pointed to Kim's throat and then the floor. He indicated his own throat and waved toward the ceiling.

"Right," said Kim. "Difference in vocal chord structure. But wait a minute. I can correct that. What a dum-dum I am."

"You sure are," agreed Toby Lee. "Get a throat microphone with frequency settings and adjust it until you get a mutually understood sound. Of course the language may be a problem."

"Don't think so. All the cities had a common language. In fact, all mankind shared a common language even before the nukie wars. This fella is a man, remember, produced by men, remember."

Kim worked swiftly, setting the broken forepaw and sheathing it in the flexible yet position-locking gelatin, the algin made from sea kelp. He pointed to his own mouth and opened it, then he touched the otter-man's.

It gaped exposing a formidable array of sharp, flesh-rending teeth. Kim popped a pill into it and grinned as it vanished.

"I wouldn't take a pill from anybody I didn't know," sniffed Toby Lee.

"He knows I want to help him."

"He'll find out."

"And right now," said Kim, padding over to the com console, and rooting in one of the small equipment drawers until he found two throat mikes. He placed one against the otter-man's throat and put his good paw up to hold it in place. He held the other against his own.

"How do you feel?" he asked, shoving the adjustment up to its highest frequency range level.

He reached out and set the other mike to its lowest frequency transmission range.

"I am not in pain," declared a high, yet not unpleasantly so, voice. "And my thanks for your care."

"You saved our lives," said Kim.

"And you mine. How are you called?"

"I am Kim. My companion is Toby. And you?"

"I am called Kirl, as are all members of my group, which is called Kirl. You are of the people who died? The Forerunners? Those who stayed as they were? We have seen you in the sea, and we fear you. We do not think you mean the ocean to be free.

"Now help me to the water. It must be decided whether you may stay." There was pain in the brown eyes. "Many things must be decided."

"I will come with you and help you to your friends," said Kim.

"And you may not come back," added Toby Lee.

"Then wait a decent length of time, button up the boat, and go. But wait. Sooner or later this mission has to be reported, and you know it. Further, and somewhere along the line, we have to look for Genright and Tuk as well if the earth's stopped shaking out there.

"I'm taking the mikes and a few belt things with me."

Kirl spoke. "You are asking the Toby one to stay behind in this . . . ?"

"Boat," said Kim, speaking into the mike. "And I am."

The otter-man heaved erect and stood on his rear legs much as the hydronauts had seen another stand on whale back in the moonlight. Kim helped him scramble up the hatch to the curved deck. Together they slid into the water and swam for the rocky shore line. And as they did so, a shrill, vibrating, audible whistling arose from the sea people on the rocks and penetrated their skulls. Toby held her hands over her ears, and Kim shook his head.

10

Kim returned to *Adam 1* alone. He was disturbed and thoughtful although he managed a flashing smile for Tuktu and Genright.

"What took you so long?" he asked. "And why did you bring your preserved friends?"

"They fell off a wall," said Genright.

"Stop it," demanded Toby, her voice breaking. "And talk."

Seated within *Adam 1*, and with the deck hatch pulled tight above them, Kim did so.

"I may not have this all clear," he said, "but Kirl, the sea person who led us here, is a leader of a group called Kirl, the otter-people who make this place their home. They call themselves the Ocean Ones. I gather this means the entire race."

"They don't know they're otters?" asked Genright.

"They aren't," snapped Toby. "They're . . . uh, ah . . ."

"The Ocean Ones," Tuktu said gravely.

"Men in a form designed for sea survival, created by men to assure some sort of a future for humanity," said Kim softly.

"In any case, there are other communities of Ocean People besides the Kirl, all of them the same physically, I gather, but each group located in other parts of the world in hide-outs much like this one, perhaps.

"Now, again I'm not sure of this," he continued, "but the race split after the birthing hatch apparently under some sort of implanted genetic instruction to divide. And each group had instructions to find its own home, a home or place that had been prepared in advance for it.

"I mean that while the laboratory experts were creating the hatch, other men either were exploring or had worked out a set of localities where the race would have a maximum chance to survive."

"Whew!" muttered Genright.

"Picked a mighty risky seismic location for this home," said Tuktu.

"Right," snapped Kim. "And because the people of the hives wouldn't think it livable even when the hot earth cooled enough for men.

"But they did more, those scientific ancestors of ours. They left a means of education and a store of knowledge at each location so the Ocean People could grow and progress to the best of their abilities in the environment which confronted them.

"There is a vast cavern not far from us. That's where Kirl took me, and where I met with five other Kirls, sort of a council. And a part of that cavern is a laboratory library complete with pictures of people like us. The Ocean People call them the Forerunners."

"You mean that the Kirl know their own history?" asked Toby softly.

"And much of ours as well."

There was a moment of silence.

Tuktu broke it. "Well," he said, "if they

showed you all that, it means that they intend to be friendly."

"Not at all," said Kim. "I think I was given as much information as I could absorb because they don't intend for us to leave this place."

He banged his thigh with the flat of his hand.

"Kirl knows we're tied to the sub. He certainly knows that Genright and Tuktu are here, and even that Cryos are floating around outside. But anyhow, Genright, you and Tuk are going to go out that bottom bubble hatch wearing silco suits and jet mantles to try a trip through the tunnel again. Take the com equipment and make a report. Just get as much information on the open bands as possible.

"You may not make it at all, but we have to try."

"Lots of otters out there," said Genright as he suited for the trip.

"Lots of them watching us too," muttered Tuktu.

"Maybe not yet," Kim said evenly. "As soon as you leave, Toby and I are going topside to be real visible. Maybe do something about the Cryos."

"I wouldn't," said Toby.

"Well, maybe not now, but we can unload the sled. We're going to need all the gear."

"If we don't get back, you'll know we were picked up by the *Polaris*," said Tuktu.

"Oh, we'll be right along. I like it here," grinned Genright.

Kim closed the bubble hatch behind them.

Dusk, if it comes at all, comes late in the high latitudes. There was plenty of light as Toby Lee and Kim unloaded the sled and packed its contents into the hull of *Adam I*. But there were deep shadows on the water of the vast expanse of lake that poured itself away into the fastnesses of the mountain rings. The peaks closed away much of the sky, but the slanting sun bathing their summits made them seem like a ring of torches. Some of them, indeed, smoked, but from their own internal fires.

"Nothing swims faster or better than the sea otters," said Toby.

"They are not equipped to climb," muttered Kim, his eyes on the horizon and the jumbled heights. "They trot around on those rocks pretty nimbly though."

"Oh, I like them," said Toby, "really like them."

"You swim pretty well yourself," said Kim. "Trot around on rocks pretty fine too."

"You like me?"

"Loads, bundles, tons . . ."

"Then why are you frowning and looking at the shore?"

"May be a messenger from there with a message."

"Like let's get some sleep?"

"Something like that. After you, Warden Three."

"You're trying to make me stop worrying."

"Something like that, partly maybe."

"I'll rub your back."

"Be very nice, I'm sure."

Genright and Tuktu moved steadily through the tunnel against the incoming current yet with a good rate of speed, with the jet mantles giving them extra thrust.

They set suit lights to a minimum, using just enough glow for visibility. They held conversation to companionable grunts. They concentrated on swimming, and being superb athletes, they even made small bow waves against their chests.

They noticed that along some portions of the tunnel the inrushing water did not completely fill the entire bore, that at the top of the stream in those areas there was air, breathable air.

They drove steadily forward.

"Water's warmer," said Genright.

"Swim."

Their lights broke the silhouette of the tunnel ahead of them. They switched to a higher beam intensity and picked out the tiny hole in the closed end, their entrance.

And they heard the swirl of disturbed water behind them. They were overtaken.

"I'm dropping off with the stun rods," said Tuktu. "You get out and make the run for shore."

"Don't kill. Just slow 'em if you can."

Genright was gone, and Tuktu was in a tangle of most energetic otter-men. Two of them boiled past him after Genright. He sprayed his weapon tube at random, and three of the creatures shuddered to a limp halt. He dropped the tube and helped one of them, swimming for the tunnel roof and the hope of air. The others not in pursuit of Genright lifted the other two. Tuktu was trapped in huge otter bodies. He had the certain knowledge that any one of his captors could just as easily have bitten one of his legs off.

Genright, skinny Genright, slithered through tunnel end, jetted for the surface, and with the mantles pulsing and impelling him at high speed, made the rocky shore while his pursuit was still in the oily surf. He kicked off fins in one rapid motion and ran for a break in the cliff. He found handholds, warm ones, for the land was still warm and scrambled upward.

The Ocean People, two of them, stood on hind legs and watched him climb.

Genright climbed until he found a ledge nearly a hundred feet above the bay. He rested, and as he did so, he examined the communications equipment. It was fine.

Not as fine as that in *Adam 1,* however. Then why go to all this trouble? Why didn't Kim get a message out? Why, indeed, knucklehead, he thought. He looked at the crag above him. The lake inside the mountain lay at the bottom of a deep crater, and the peaks held it embraced on all sides. Maybe an aircraft of some sort could pluck a laser-beamed radio message from that jumble of interference. Maybe. He had no doubt that Kim had already tried to get word out. Okay, so maybe also, he had some doubt as he realized that Kim and Toby must have known they would be in trouble with the Service. He was not there to speculate.

Genright settled down to his work, the work of the Service and his assigned mission. He spoke to the open band and told his story completely and succinctly. He was halfway through it again when the *Polaris* cut into his narrative.

Commander Brent spoke. "Start once more, Genright," he said calmly, "and from when you last reported from the beachhead. We are recording now on all units.

"Frankly, the *Polaris* has suffered some seismic beating too, but nothing serious that can't be fixed reasonably soon."

Genright told it all again. This time he remembered to mention the Cryos floating in the lake. He also mentioned that the cliff at his back seemed to be heating again.

"Fine," said Commander Brent. "We have it all. Now can you change to another frequency? You know the one."

"Yes, sir," answered Genright, examining his helmet transmitter settings. "I am now on it."

"Good. Give me as much as you can about the numbers of Kirl, or your Ocean People. Any indications of their sciences, any sign of weapons, any evidence of formal habitat, any notion of possible vehicles, anything at all to round out Kim's report of his meeting with the Kirl council."

"I have nothing firm on those matters, sir. I don't even know how many of the Ocean People I saw in the lake. Maybe a few hundred, as a guess. There could be thousands more along other portions of the lake, which is a considerable body of water that may run many miles."

"But you think your party is now in definite danger and could be eliminated?"

Genright peeked down at the strip of beach below him.

"I was sure of it a minute ago, sir."

"What does that mean, boy?" The Commander had apparently abandoned discipline. "Either your lives are at stake or they are not."

"Let me put it this way, sir. I told you Tuktu had been taken in the tunnel to give me a chance to get out. I assumed that he had been damaged or made captive and taken back.

"But now I see him with the otter-men."

There was frustrated fury in Commander Brent's voice.

"What is he doing, you black and white nuisance?"

"He seems to be helping the Ocean People to drag two of their number up on the beach, and he's now giving one of them artificial respiration. At least he has his mask over the otter-man's muzzle and is giving him oxygen.

"Yes sir, that fella is stirring and moving. Tuktu's doing the same for the other one. Everybody seems pleased."

"Warden Two, I am turning this over to Commander Torrance for a moment. I feel somewhat confused."

"Genright Selsor, you listen real hard," snapped Commander Tod Torrance. "You mean that you are viewing a peaceful scene? That Tuktu is well, and sort of one of the boys, as it were?"

"Exactly, sir. And I am going down to mingle myself as soon as Commander Brent tells me what to tell Kim about the Cryos."

"Stay right where you are. We're not finished with your report. I'll have a senior psyke in to tell you about the Cryos. They are most tricky to handle, and some of them have to be destroyed. Meanwhile we are assuming that you intend to return to that lake with the Ocean People . . . ?"

"Yes, sir, Tuk and me. I can't hang on a cliff that keeps hotting up forever, and I don't know of any other place to go except open sea."

Commander Jiggs Jensen spoke, his soft voice even softer.

"Tell you true, Genright. The *Polaris* might not be able to travel for a few days. We couldn't come in to pick you up even if we knew exactly where to try for you under the circumstances. We have your fixes, sure, and we'll act on them later.

"It might be a lot later. Commander Brent has his superior officers too, and he'll have to make a complete report to them on this most important matter. But remember, for what it's worth, your mission was a success despite the trouble you're all in. A new race of man verified . . . an Ocean

People . . . Do what you think is best, and tell Rockwell he's still in command. Here's your senior psyke about the Cryos. If he tells you to do nothing, do it. If he tells you what to do, do it exactly."

He chuckled somewhat sadly. "You're dealing with the forerunners of the Forerunners, son. Not stable people at all."

Commander Brent's voice interrupted.

"Here are your orders. I know these will be obeyed for a change. You are to rejoin the Ocean People and your companions. You will endure, survive, and report when possible. This area, your area, will be monitored, by fish guts, forever."

"Yes sir," said Genright. "I'm going down to join ol' Tuk and his friends. Out, sirs."

He clambered down the cliff, missed a foothold near the bottom, and thudded to the beach on his back. One of the otter-men galloped over and sniffed at him, then showed him a vast mouth full of sharp teeth.

"You looked mighty silly up there like a cormorant, skinny buddy," said Tuktu.

"You've got a bang over your right eye I'm glad to say," muttered Genright.

There was a dull, booming convulsion in the bay. The otter-men squealed and entered the sea.

The hydronauts checked out suits and followed them.

The entire band was well into the tunnel when a shock wave of water spurted them forward and a dull, vibrating thud made ears ring.

"There goes the entrance for good, I think," said Tuktu into his com unit.

"I'm getting plenty sick of this old tunnel anyhow," fluted Genright. "And all that glacier scenery gives me the crawlies."

"Don't think we'll see much more of it for a long time."

"Be other things to do."

"Right."

Toby Lee and Kim were on the tiny hatch deck of *Adam I* when their escort returned them to the work sub. Kirl was with them, his forepaw and leg at ease in the gel splint as he used it to hold the throat mike.

The escort made its report to Kirl as Kim listened in to that sound above sound. Each of their faces were serious, then pleased.

Kirl spoke to Kim.

"You will be of us now for much time."

"For much time," said Kim thoughtfully, his gaze thrusting over the lake to where the junior icebergs and their cargoes bobbed placidly.

The hydronauts sat and looked at the lake for

hours after the Kirl had gone ashore, probably once more to parley their fate with the Ocean People. Toby Lee and Kim held hands. Tuktu looked at Genright as though he'd never seen him.

It was quiet in the great crater, and there was serenity over the faraway peaks.

Kim spoke for all of them.

"What do you know," he said. "We've got a new home, a new people to learn, new manners, customs, language, terrain, and, I think, we try to revive the Cryos just to complicate matters. But you know something else? We made our mission."

"That's what Jiggs Jensen said."

"Who's he?" asked Tuktu.

"Do you see what I see?" asked Toby Lee.

Out on the lake there was a great ripple, and a monstrous back humped into view. Two measly fountains lifted from a mottled head.

"That whale's landlocked," said Tuktu.

"Tube Steak, you big sneak in the pay of a bunch of sea otters, come over here and bring your yellow rump with you," shouted Genright. He gazed sternly at his companions. "I don't want any of you guys messing around with my whale."

CARL L. BIEMILLER has long been a familiar name to magazine readers, and to a continually growing audience of juvenile fiction fans. He has been a journalist most of his life, a former assistant publisher of the Camden *Courier-Post* and the Philadelphia *Daily News*, a long time executive editor of Holiday Magazine. He lives on the New Jersey coast within the sound of the surf, and his interest in oceanography is always at high tide. He works today in the public relations business between books. When this one was written he was serving as public relations director for the City of Atlantic City, and planning another volume for his HYDRONAUT series.